Mason Caught Her Face Between His Hands— Forcing Her To Meet His Gaze.

Then, suddenly, her body was empty of his possession.

"No! Please, don't stop now." Helena begged as Mason pulled away from her and got up from the bed. "What's wrong?"

Under his cool scrutiny Helena felt reduced to little more than a butterfly on a pin. She desperately wished she could cover her naked body from the emptiness in his gaze.

"There's nothing wrong." His answer was delivered at subzero temperature.

"Then why? Why did you stop?"

"Because I can." He tossed her clothes on the bed. The inference in his action was clear. Get dressed and get the hell out of his room. "And because now I know how far you're prepared to go."

Dear Reader,

Sometimes our lives are touched by the people in them without us even realizing the long-term impact they have on us. I grew up half a world away from extended family but had the pleasure of the company of a grandmotherly neighbour who introduced me to reading romance when I hit my teens. Those books ignited a love of romance in me, a fire, that still burns as fiercely now as it did back then—a fire that compels me to write stories like the Knight brothers' journeys to love.

In one of my previous jobs I traveled as a sales representative through the central North Island of New Zealand. The winter roads can be treacherous, the isolation during the journey overwhelming—yet help can be just around the next corner in the road from a source as yet unknown. When I originally started writing *The Tycoon's Hidden Heir,* the third in my New Zealand Knights trilogy, I was motivated by the possible chain of events after a chance encounter triggered by a near-death experience. The what ifs were mind-boggling.

I hope you enjoy Mason and Helena's story and that it keeps your love of romance burning bright.

With warmest wishes,

Yvonne Lindsay

YVONNE LINDSAY

THE TYCOON'S HIDDEN HEIR

Published by Silhouette Books
America's Publisher of Contemporary Romance

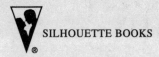 SILHOUETTE BOOKS

ISBN-13: 978-0-373-76788-5
ISBN-10:   0-373-76788-9

THE TYCOON'S HIDDEN HEIR

Visit Silhouette Books at www.eHarlequin.com

Printed in U.S.A.

Books by Yvonne Lindsay

Silhouette Desire

*The Boss's Christmas Seduction #1758
*The CEO's Contract Bride #1776
*The Tycoon's Hidden Heir #1788

*New Zealand Knights

YVONNE LINDSAY

New Zealand born to Dutch immigrant parents, Yvonne Lindsay became an avid romance reader at the age of thirteen. Now, married to her "blind date" and with two surprisingly amenable teenagers, she remains a firm believer in the power of romance. Yvonne balances her days between a part-time legal management position and crafting the stories of her heart. In her spare time, when not writing, she can be found with her nose firmly in a book, reliving the power of love in all walks of life. She can be contacted via her Web site, www.yvonnelindsay.com.

To Robyn Donald and Daphne Clair
for their support in the darkest hours,
for creating Kara School of Writing
for people just like me
and for sharing the joy when dreams come true!

Prologue

Twelve years ago...

Black, ice-cold water swirled around her, sapping the last of the heat from her body, the last of her will to survive. A tinge of irony touched her mind that she should die this way. Helena Milton, full of life, colour and crazy dreams, and powered by a get-go attitude to life that had alternately amazed and dismayed her quieter elderly parents.

Her parents—would they ever understand why she'd left? Why she'd agreed to marry Patrick Davies and settle for less than love? Deep in her heart she knew she was doing the right thing—for herself, sure, but most of all for them and for the sacrifices they'd made for her.

But she'd failed. An uncontrollable skid on the ice- and snow-strewn road had plunged her car through the bridge barrier and into the swollen river below. The river which now flumed with chilled water from the melting snow that came straight off New Zealand's central plateau mountains.

Helena lifted numbed frozen fingers to try the switch for the electric windows again. Futile. Not even her ever-weakened attempts to break the glass had any effect. With the doors jammed and the car's electrics out of commission she remained trapped. Helena closed her eyes again. What was the point in keeping them open when all around her was nothing but blackness?

A spark of anger lit briefly in her chest that she could die like this—alone and with her goals unfulfilled, no chance to earn her father's pride instead of being the object of his quiet disappointment. Defeat had an ugly, bitter taste.

Let go, whispered the little voice at the back of her head. *Let go.* She sagged deeper into her car seat, accepting the cold that penetrated to her bones, and let her mind drift. How long would it take, she wondered.

A new and different sound from outside penetrated the thickening fog of reluctant acceptance in her mind. She forced her eyelids up and scanned around her. Fairy lights on the road above. A crazed laugh, broken and weak, choked from her throat as some of her usual humour surfaced. Whatever happened to the white light at the end of the tunnel everyone talked about?

A dark figure loomed at her driver's window, a pale face pressed against the glass. Water foamed around the figure and against the window's edge. Helena felt the car shift slightly with the increasing pressure of the river's pummelling force. The man's lips moved but she shook her head slowly in response.

What was he saying? His arms raised and she recognised the outline of an axe clenched in his hands. He tapped it against the glass. Helena suddenly understood what he'd been trying to say. She threw herself sideways, into the deepening pool in her car, oblivious to the dice-shaped pieces of broken safety glass that showered her body.

The roaring growl of the water, muffled before, now crashed intrusively against her ears. Strong hands reached in to grab her by her jacket, her hair, anything that gave her rescuer purchase. Helena struggled to help him as he dragged her through the gaping window but she flopped uselessly as her limbs refused to obey. With one powerful lift he manoeuvred her slight frame free from the car. The shield of his body protected her from the hungry determination of the swirling current as he carried her to the bank.

The bank was hard, blessedly so. Helena relished each pressure point of discomfort as confirmation she still lived. She'd been so close to giving in. The concept that she was finally safe rejoiced through her mind. Now, all she wanted to do was sleep, except the man who'd pulled her from the car seemed determined not to let her.

"Is there anyone else in the car?" her rescuer shouted in her ear. "C'mon! Answer me, is there anyone else?"

Slowly, her lips formed the words, her voice weak. "No. Alone."

"Thank God. Are you hurt? Did you lose consciousness?"

She felt his hands, strong and capable, probe her scalp then skim her body as she shook her head. The cold air bit through her wet clothing all the way to her bones.

"Doesn't look like you've broken anything. Let's get you somewhere dry."

"My things? My car?" she managed to ask through frozen lips.

"Sorry, hon. Your car's heading downstream. First order of business is to get you dry and warm."

Her rescuer lifted her into his arms and strode toward what she now recognised as a large truck and trailer unit parked in a lay-by to the side of the road. A tiny smile pulled at her lips as she recognised the source of her earlier confusion. A long-distance trucker, his rig was festooned with driving lights.

"What's so funny?"

His voice was deep, young. Reassuring. She wanted to see what he looked like but the effort required to tilt her head and pick out his profile in the shadows cast by the truck's lights remained beyond her.

"Fairy lights," she whispered.

A deep chuckle rumbled through his body. "Sure, fairy lights."

He lifted her up into the cab of his truck then climbed in after her to settle her into the basic sleeping compartment behind.

"Do you remember how long you were in the water? What time you crashed?"

"J-just after nine…I think."

He flung a look at the clock on the dash. "About half an hour then. What the hell were you doing out on the road without chains? Didn't you see the warning signs?"

"D-didn't w-want to stop. I have to get to Auckland." The short speech took every last ounce of energy left within her.

"You won't be going anywhere tonight."

A sudden disembodied voice on the radio elicited a sharp curse from her rescuer before he responded. She tried to listen, catching only the words *accident* and *hypothermia* before drowsiness pulled at her with the strength of a super magnet. She began to slide into unconsciousness, rousing only as he shook her gently.

"Hey, don't go to sleep yet. You have to get those clothes off and get warm again. Can you manage?"

"N-no. F-fingers t-too cold."

She felt as helpless as a rag doll when he began to peel off her wet clothing, muttering under his breath as her limp limbs hindered the process and massive tremors racked her body.

"Shivering, that's good. You're on your way back."

Pain seared through her as circulation sluggishly resumed. "B-b-back? I n-never got where I was g-going."

He chuckled again, and Helena decided she liked the sound. It was deep and warm and made her feel alive again. Alive—something she'd taken for granted for far too long.

"I hate to tell you this, but we're stuck here for the night. I'd hoped we could make it farther up the line to a motel but the authorities have closed the roads in both directions until morning."

As soon as she was naked he laid her gently, almost clinically, on her side on the narrow bunk and tucked a down-filled sleeping bag around her body. She vaguely heard the sounds of his own wet clothing slap onto the floor. She couldn't stop shivering and the sleeping bag slid away from her body, exposing the length of her back. She barely felt the mattress dip as he lay down beside her but the heat that radiated from his body was seductively welcome. She sighed as strong-muscled arms gathered her close against the rock-hard plane of his chest and was asleep before he settled the sleeping bag around them both.

It was still dark when Mason Knight woke, disoriented, to find a warm, slender and very naked female body on top of his. The crush of her breasts against his chest and the tangle of her legs in his brought him to full aching arousal. Disorientation fled as he remembered the rescue from the car stuck in the rising river and bringing the driver to the truck to get her warm. Standard survival procedure, he reminded himself—get naked, get dry, get warm—but nothing in his survival training during his stint in the New Zealand army had prepared him for this particular scenario.

He willed his body into submission but one part of his anatomy stubbornly ignored him. Slowly and deliberately he poured images through his mind designed to quell even the hottest ardour—no luck.

He tried to shift his hips and roll her to one side against the back wall of the sleeper but she squirmed against him—the central core of her body so close to him he could feel the heat that now emanated from that private part of her. Shit. She'd freak out if she woke now, and he sure wouldn't blame her.

Shock jolted through his body as small feminine hands stroked feather-light across his torso, sending wild coils of desire tightening in ever-decreasing spirals. She rubbed her cheek against his chest, a sigh escaping her lips to brush over his sensitised skin.

"I need you." Her voice was husky and travelled through the velvet midnight darkness like a caress.

"No, it's just reaction to the accident. You're in

shock." In shock? *He* was the one in shock. "You don't want to do this."

"I need this. I need you." Her lips found one of his nipples and her tongue swirled around the sensitive flat disk, sending a raging hunger through his body that didn't want to take no for an answer. "Show me I'm alive," she whispered as she pressed her hips against his hungry flesh, a sharp moan punctuating her demand.

She rose up onto her knees—deft hands reaching for him, stroking his iron-hard shaft, her fingertips barely touching the swollen head, guiding him to the source of her heat—then she sank down onto him with a throaty groan that almost saw him lose control right there and then. A massive tremor rippled through her body as she took his full length deep within her and she stilled, her hands now resting on his shoulders. Then, she began to rock, slowly tilting her pelvis back and forth, maintaining the searing contact between their bodies, heat and moisture building between them like molten lava.

Mason trailed his fingers over her thighs and to her hips where he grasped a firm hold of her, silently encouraging her to up the tempo as his hips thrust upward to meet her every stroke.

This was crazy—he was crazy to let her do this—but somehow, in the anonymity of the dark night hours, it seemed as if it was the only right thing left in the world. To think that all her vitality, her heat, could have been gone forever. Yeah, he understood her need to affirm life—to feel life—right now.

Right. Now.

His climax hit him with the force of a runaway train and his fingers bit into her skin as he pumped against her. Her sharp cry of completion and the rhythmic pull of her muscles as they contracted around him prolonged the ecstasy even as she collapsed against him, shaking with the aftermath of pleasure.

"Thank you," she whispered, her head resting against his chest where his heart pounded so hard he thought any second now it would leap right from his chest. He cleared his throat to speak, but she raised one finger and pressed it against his lips. "Shh, don't say anything." And then, just like that, she was fast asleep again.

Aftershocks continued to quiver through his body. Mason hooked his arms about her and cradled her to him as he'd never held another woman before. In this timeless moment she was his woman and his alone. The overwhelming urge to claim her and protect her from the world came from out of nowhere—strong, feral, invincible. What the hell was he thinking? He didn't even know her name! Who was she? What kind of woman was she, that she could make love with such abandon to a total stranger then fall asleep in his arms as if she belonged nowhere else?

By the time the wintry-grey fingers of dawn crept across the sky he was no closer to finding his answers. Silent and careful, he eased her from his body, watching as she instinctively nestled into the warmth of the depression where he'd lain. He stifled an oath as his toes made contact with the near-frozen wet clothing abandoned on the floor and quickly reached for clean dry jeans and a sweatshirt from the locker above the bed.

A quick check on the radio confirmed the roads had been declared safe enough to reopen. It was time to go. He had a lot of time to make up and a wedding to get to in Auckland later that afternoon. His boss was much older than his bride-to-be and had been alternately ridiculed and lauded in the tabloids about his forthcoming nuptials. Either way, Mason didn't give a damn, but he did respect the man who'd given him his first job out of the army and had begun to teach him everything he knew about the transport industry in New Zealand. Mason considered it an honour to stand up for him when his boss's adult son from his first marriage had point-blank refused to have anything to do with the wedding.

The rustle of bedclothes in the sleeper drew his attention back to his immediate problem.

"The roads are open again," he said over his shoulder, reluctant to make eye contact.

"That's good. Is there a chance I can borrow something of yours to wear until my clothes dry out?"

"Sure, just check the locker. There's a spare belt in there somewhere, too."

"Thanks."

He felt her pause, as if weighing up the wisdom of bringing up last night. She'd obviously reached the same conclusion he had—ignore it and just maybe it would fade away. Every muscle in his shoulders clenched and he gripped the steering wheel with white-knuckled fingers as he listened to her pull on some clothes. The thought of his clothes clinging to the satin-soft creaminess of her skin had him rock hard in a split second. He fought the urge to turn around and watch her. Did her body clamour to repeat their nocturnal experience in the cold light of day as loudly as his did?

Apparently not. Eventually she came forward and plopped down into the passenger's seat in the cab and he got his first real look at her.

Hell, she barely looked twenty. Delicate fingers combed through tousled, long brown hair, hair that in the streaks of early sunlight reflected reddish lights of burnished copper. Delicate fingers that had held him last night, had guided him inside her body. His gut clenched into a fiery ball of want and he forced his eyes forward to the frozen landscape that stretched ahead of them, not willing to see what lay in her green eyes, not wanting to commit the pale heart-shaped face to his memory. But it was already too late. He would never forget her. Not her scent, not her touch—nothing.

"Thanks. For everything." Her voice was husky, hesitant, as if she found the words difficult to say.

"You're welcome," he ground out through teeth that ached, they were clenched so hard together. He forced his gaze back out the windscreen. It was clear she regretted her impulsiveness already. Okay, he could be a gentleman. He could ignore last night and the clawing need that the mere sight of her aroused in him. Somehow. "So, where are you headed?"

"Auckland, but you can drop me at the nearest town. I need to make a phone call first."

"That's it then?"

He heard her breath catch in her throat, just the slightest hitch, but quite enough to tell him she'd understood his question fully. Her answer was softly spoken but rang with finality as she turned to stare out the passenger window. "Yes, that's it."

Mason ran a finger inside the stiff white collar of his shirt and loosened his tie another blessed millimetre. All day he'd been plagued by last night's memories. Finally, while he was getting ready for the wedding, he'd resolved to try to find out who she was. The registration of her wrecked car would be a good start once it was dragged from the river. A few calls would do it. Then he would track her down—to see if they could make something more of the incendiary passion they'd shared. He'd never known anything like it. Like her. He wanted to know more.

He thought of what he'd gotten up to as a teenager to rile his dad and of the five years he'd spent in the army—of how he'd constantly searched for that one thing that would make his life feel like it had a purpose. The one thing to fill the void he himself couldn't define. For a brief time that void had been filled last night. He had to find her. He had to know if she was what he'd been looking for.

Patrick gave him a nudge as the opening strains of the wedding march drew the assembled congregation to their feet in unison. A hush settled amongst the crowd as the bride began her journey down the thickly carpeted centre aisle in Auckland's oldest and largest city church. All heads turned for their first look at the wife-to-be of one of New Zealand's wealthiest men and for the first time in his life Mason Knight nearly blacked out as his midnight lover glided down the aisle.

One

"It's quite simple, Helena. If you don't assign control of Brody's half share of the business to me within the next thirty days I will take every step to ensure the world knows exactly how you and my father met. Let's see how your precious son copes at school once everyone knows that juicy titbit."

He knew? How on earth had he found out? Helena's stomach lurched. Despite how careful she'd been to conceal her past, it was something she'd known could come out of the woodwork anytime in the last twelve years. That it should be from Patrick's eldest son, Evan, shouldn't have come as a surprise.

Her heart ached for Brody. He had only just settled back at his exclusive boarding school and had been

troubled since Patrick's sudden death—easily upset and
reluctant to leave her. Understandable, all of it, of
course. She was already worried about how he'd cope
at school during this difficult period of adjustment. If
Evan spread his poisonous secret Brody's life would
become a living hell. She would not let that happen.

But what on earth was she to do? Already entrenched
in the company as marketing director, from the day of
Patrick's fatal heart attack, Evan had exerted his power
as new part owner of Davies Freight and taken over
Patrick's chair and the decision-making processes that
fell to the managing director. She'd been unable to stop
him, and with the demands of dealing with Brody's
grief, not to mention her own, she hadn't had the energy
left to fight back in the boardroom. This week, she'd
finally returned to the office, where she supervised the
business's administration. It hadn't taken long to
discover Evan had completely taken over.

Evan had never appreciated or understood his father's
love of the cut and thrust of the industry, or his cautious
plans for expansion. No, all he saw was an easy ticket
to maintain his plush lifestyle and the quickest way to
get rid of her. Of course, on paper, he could be seen to
have gone through the motions—pitching new contracts,
renewing old ones—but deeper analysis had shown the
truth. If Evan was permitted to keep on his current path
the business would be bankrupt within a year.

She'd grown up having to scrape together every penny.
There was no way she would let that happen to her son.

A look of scorn slid across her stepson's face, making
it patently clear that no matter how coldly polite he'd
been to her while his father was alive, the gloves were
most definitely off now. Helena's fingernails bit into her

palms as she struggled not to whack him hard across his smug features. No doubt he hoped she'd do exactly that. With his connections, he could press assault charges and see her son removed from her care. Then he could do whatever he wanted with Brody's share of the company. Yeah, he'd like that all right, but it sure wouldn't happen this side of hell freezing over. Not while she still had breath in her body.

What scared her most was if Evan discovered the full truth he'd delight in ripping his much younger half brother to shreds. With the resources he had at his disposal she knew he'd have people digging for dirt on her—the fact he'd found out how she and Patrick had met was just one example of how far he was prepared to go to find anything to discredit her and help him reach his avaricious goal. She had to protect her son, no matter what, and at the same time to somehow find the courage to honour Patrick's last wishes to the letter.

Helena swallowed back the tears that threatened. When she'd met Patrick she'd been prepared to accept his help in return for her companionship in marriage. She'd never dreamed she would learn to love him. She missed her husband more than she could ever have imagined— his steady hand on the tiller of their world, his gentle encouragement to strive for her dreams, his unadulterated enjoyment in the child born within the first year of their marriage. He'd always boasted Brody had made him young again. Not young enough, unfortunately, to see the fast-growing boy much past eleven years old.

"So?" Evan's sneer jerked her back to cold harsh reality. "What do you say?"

"I can't answer you now, Evan. It's too soon."

"Don't underestimate me, Helena. You and the brat

are just a blip on my radar. I'll leave now, but remember I will have what's my due—one way or another."

Helena couldn't bring herself to rise from her chair to even see him from her home, couldn't trust herself not to resort to the old Helena and to fly at him, giving vent to her rage. No, if there was one thing she'd learned the hard way in the past twelve years it was to think first, act second. Evan knew the way out; she only wished he'd stay there.

The hollow echo of the front door resounded through the house and the tension slowly ebbed from her shoulders. God, she'd thought she was tough but it would take more than tough to see her through this. It would take a miracle. She drew in a deep breath and rose from the chair. There was work to be done, and plenty of it. First, she had to arrange an appointment—one she'd been dreading. She couldn't ignore Patrick's final instructions any longer.

Her heart twisted with regret that her sweet, generous husband had understood the reality of his eldest son's true nature, that he'd known that this situation would come to pass.

Half an hour later Helena let the telephone receiver fall back haphazardly into its cradle. Mason Knight was nigh on impossible to track down. She couldn't give up though, he was the one man Patrick had said would be able to help her, the one man he'd insisted she ask and, coincidentally, the last man on earth she wanted to seek out for help.

The secretary at his office had said he was out of Auckland and refused to give any further information, but Patrick had mentioned something about a holiday home on the Coromandel that Mason used as his bolthole when he needed to escape the city. She'd lay odds on him being there, so that's where she had to go.

A warning trickle of dread ran down her spine and for a moment Helena questioned whether she was doing the right thing. As intimately as they'd known one another that one and only time, the man was a virtual stranger. How would he react when she turned up on his doorstep and asked for help? Over the years he'd made it perfectly clear to her how much he detested her, and had avoided seeing Patrick when she too would be there.

Could she stand it if he slammed the door in her face and left her to deal with Evan on her own? And what of Brody?

There was only one thing for it. She had to get to the isolated Coromandel Peninsula address she'd found in Patrick's Rolodex. For a minute she rued the fact that Mason Knight couldn't have built his minipalace somewhere like Pauanui, a popular playground for New Zealand's wealthy and somewhere she was familiar with. But it was probably best not to have any chance of being recognised in his presence. It wouldn't take much mental arithmetic before tongues would start to wag and minds to speculate. She couldn't do that to Brody, no matter what.

Mason looked through the wall of floor-length glass that faced out to the ocean and drank in the wild beauty of the scene. He loved this place and not just because it was his own personal testament to the first million he'd ever made. He'd never grow tired of the sight of the native bush, as it hugged the hillside on its gentle drop toward the sea, or the sea's ever-changing mood. It'd been too long since he'd come here to recharge.

When he woken at 5:00 a.m., his mind still fogged with sleep, he'd known it was time to clear his diary and get away from the city, and all its demands, for the weekend. Okay, so it had taken some juggling, and a few extra grey hairs for his secretary, but he'd walked out of the office at two-thirty this afternoon without a backward glance. Now the weekend stretched before him, gloriously empty. His to do with whatever the hell he wanted.

He lifted a glass of red wine in a silent toast to the view then put it to his lips and relished the flavour of his favourite merlot—an indulgence he saved only for these stolen weekends here at his hideaway. His mouth twisted into a wry smile. Of course, Patrick had always teased him that the only thing to make a runaway weekend perfect was spending it in the company of a special person. But Mason had no such special person in his life. He had neither the time nor the inclination to weed through the gold diggers, the publicity seekers, the schemers.

Realistically, of course, he knew that not all women were like that—his sisters-in-law being perfect examples and hell-bent on putting what they believed were suitable marriageable candidates across his path. What was it about happily married people that made them want to see everyone in the same state, he wondered. It was like an epidemic over the past couple of years. His eyes rested briefly on the snapshot of his growing extended family taken at their last gathering. Who would've thought he'd be an uncle twice over by now?

Marriage. His lip curled slightly at the thought. While his brothers, Declan and Connor, didn't seem to have any complaints it certainly wasn't a state he was in any hurry to embrace. What he enjoyed now was the company of suitable escorts from his personal list. Sophisticated women who made no emotional demands on him at all. Cut-and-dried—just the way he liked it.

Mason strolled across the room to flip the light switch. It grew dark early this time of year. The wind was coming up. Good. He loved a howling winter storm. Nothing like it to blow the cobwebs from your mind and reenergize your soul. He had everything here he needed, and if the power went out, so be it. Nothing would mar the perfection of his all-too-infrequent time away from work, alone.

Buzz, buzz!

Mason froze. Nothing but the intrusion of an uninvited guest, he thought as the gate intercom's strident warning bounced about the high-raftered ceiling. Who the hell could it be? He hadn't even told his secretary where he was headed when he walked out the office door. Sure, his brothers or his dad would figure this was where he'd come if they tried to contact him at home, but they would respect his privacy. One thing was for sure: whoever was at the gate wasn't welcome.

Buzz, buzz, buzzzzzzzzz!

With a muttered expletive Mason put his glass of wine down on the heavy pine coffee table and walked over to the intercom console on the far side of the room. He leaned one forearm against the wall and depressed the Talk button with a dangling finger.

"Yeah, what?" he snarled into the speaker.

"Mason? Mason Knight?"

His skin chilled as he recognised the husky lilt of the woman's voice. How the hell had she tracked him here and, more importantly, why?

"Can we talk? I really need to see you."

"We have nothing to talk about, Mrs. Davies."

"Don't switch off. It's important, or you know I wouldn't be here. Mason? Please?"

Oh yeah, she injected just the right amount of pathos into her tone. Any other man would leap to her aid. Any other man but him. But then not everyone knew what a little schemer Helena Davies was, or how little she'd valued her wedding vows. He'd often wondered just how many times she'd cuckolded Patrick since that night and the thought still made his blood boil.

"It's for Patrick. Just give me five minutes," she finished.

Mason's heart gave a twist. Patrick Davies, the one man he'd admired unreservedly—until he'd married Helena. He warred with his desire to switch off the intercom, go out onto the deck and be buffeted by the rising wind and pretend he'd never begun this conversation. But despite Patrick's appalling taste in wives, he owed it to both the man and his memory to hear her out.

"Five minutes only. Come on up."

He hit the button to unlock the gate then strode through the house to the front door and threw it open to wait for her arrival. She didn't take long. He could hear the strain of the car's engine as the transmission dropped to a lower gear to climb the steep, unsealed private road. His whole body tensed as the taxi drove onto the flagstone-covered apron outside the house.

Taxi? He stifled a groan. Only Helena Davies would bring a taxi for the two-and-a-half-hour drive from Auckland to this spot on the Coromandel. The woman threw money around like there was an unending supply. He watched as she handed a fistful of hundred-dollar notes to the driver then alighted from the vehicle. His stomach tensed. She still looked good, he noted bitterly, although a bit paler and a bit thinner than the last time he'd seen her. In the dark emerald-coloured suit, buttoned just high enough to expose a hint of perfect creamy breast, and with her brown-red hair tightly twisted to the back of her head, she played the grieving widow well.

"A taxi, Helena?"

"And what's wrong with that? I've recompensed him, and then some." Her glittering green eyes met his gaze and clashed. Every nerve in his body went on full alert.

"Just seems a bit extravagant, don't you think? Especially when you can drive any one of Patrick's cars yourself."

"I don't drive anymore. Not since… Well, anyway, I never got my confidence back behind the wheel." Her eyes drifted away from his face and fixed on a spot somewhere behind him.

Acid burned low in his belly. Like he needed the reminder of that night right now.

The taxi driver swung through the circular turning bay at the front of the house and disappeared back down the drive. *What?*

"Hey, where's he going?"

"Back to Auckland." Helena's voice held an underlying thread of steel.

The tightness in his gut ratcheted up another notch as, in a few graceful steps, she closed the distance between them. Her perfume reached out to tantalise his nostrils— a bit sweet, a bit spicy. His body stirred with unwelcome interest. He hated that she could still do that to him.

"You said five minutes." He bit the words out as if he'd chipped them from stone.

"I lied."

The conniving witch. Rage boiled up inside of him and he ground his teeth together hard to keep the heated words he wanted to shout from spilling out. She hadn't changed a bit. Now her easy source of income was gone she probably thought she could move onto her next victim. He knew her type only too well.

"Enjoy your walk home." He spun away from her and stepped back inside, but he wasn't fast enough. The telltale waft of her fragrance followed close behind.

"So call me a taxi when we're done. I don't care. I have to talk to you."

"Oh, we're done all right. Now get off my property before I have you charged for trespass."

He was unprepared for the butterfly-like touch of her hand on his arm. His skin contracted sharply under the cool softness of her fingers and he shook himself free.

"I'm sorry, Mason. I shouldn't have tricked you."

"There are a lot of things you shouldn't have done, Helena. Marrying Patrick was only one of them."

She flinched as if he'd struck her and for a split second remorse lanced through him. His mother, rest her soul, would have been ashamed to hear him speak like that to a woman—even one like Helena—but the anger he'd borne toward her, and women just like her, took a firmer grip.

"Well, neither one of us is perfect," she murmured and shivered in the rapidly cooling air.

The storm he'd predicted started to make its presence felt in the darkened sky and heavy splats of raindrops hit the pavers outside in an increasing staccato. Damn, as much as he wanted to, even he couldn't make her walk out in this.

"You'd better come in," he said begrudgingly.

He held the door open for her to pass through, showed her through to the expansive sitting room that faced out to the ocean and gestured for her to sit in a chair.

Helena looked around the room, impressed with the luxurious comfort of the large open-plan living and dining area that had obviously been structured to take advantage of what must be a spectacular view of the water in daylight. He kept the place tidy. Aside from the half-full wineglass on the coffee table there wasn't so much as a dish left out on a bench. Even the wood stack next to the fireplace was arranged with military precision.

She sat, forcing the butterflies in her stomach to calm their crazy fluttering, as Mason lifted his wine from the table and took a deliberate slow draft. He set the long-stemmed glass back on its coaster and thrust his hands deep in the pockets of his black trousers. A slight sheen of the wine lingered on his lower lip and he swept it away with the tip of his tongue. Her eyes locked onto the tiny movement and, deep inside, her muscles clenched. She forced herself to drag her eyes from his lips, from his face, and stared out at the rain that lashed against the floor-length glass windows. Darkness encroached outdoors; solar-powered lamps began to glow gently around the periphery of the deck. She stared at the lamp nearest the window until the shape blurred into a watery ball of light.

It had been a long time since she'd felt at such a disadvantage. She hated the way he deliberately tried to dominate her—forcing her to look up to him, not offering her so much as a glass of water. If it was only up to her, and if she didn't need his help so badly right now, she'd have darned well started that walk back to

Auckland and damn the consequences. But this was Brody's future, his life, and she'd crawl over broken glass if that's what it took to get Mason to help her.

Where to start, where to start? She gathered her fractured thoughts. It had been so easy when she'd mentally rehearsed this scene in the taxi during the trip down. Now, face-to-face with him, it wasn't as easy as she'd hoped.

She let her eyes briefly rake over his body. Physically she couldn't discern much change from the dark-haired stranger who'd rescued her from certain death that night—he stood at six feet tall and beneath the dark soft cotton polo shirt he still had shoulders like a world-class rugby player. But now there was a hardness to his face, a remote look to his eyes, that had never been evident in the plethora of photographs Patrick had proudly shown her of his protégé.

"Is this going to take long?" His irritated drawl dragged her attention back to the present.

"No, I'm sorry. I don't mean to waste your time. It's just…I…"

"You what?"

She'd rarely heard less interest in a question. Helena reached to the soles of her feet and hauled up all the courage she could muster. "I need your help."

"And I'd want to help you—why?" His upper lip curled in derision.

Helena forced her fingers to relax their grip on the straps of her handbag. "Because it was Patrick's last wish."

She watched as he snagged the glass with his fingers and took another pull at the wine, the slight tremor in his hand the only giveaway that, oh yes, she'd struck a chord this time. It was a low blow, she knew, using his relationship with his old mentor now, but she had to use all the ammunition at her disposal. She knew Patrick's death had hit him harder than he'd shown at the well-attended funeral six weeks ago. There he'd been locked behind an aloof façade. Polite and friendly and not a sign of any other emotion. But to her, his grief had been stark in his dark eyes, in the pallor of his face and in the tight lines that bracketed his lips. She'd ached to comfort him but knew he'd spurn any empathy from her.

"Go on." His voice was steady, his eyes cold and flat.

Helena took in a deep breath. "He told me that if I ever had a problem with Davies Freight to call on you. To ask you for help. So I am. We need you. We're in trouble, Mason."

"You're talking crap. If there was anything crumbling at Davies Freight I'd know about it. Now, if you're finished, I'll call that taxi."

Helena bit back the sharp retort that sprang to mind and took a breath before continuing, "Hear me out, please. You'll have heard that Evan took over the managing director duties. You know that was never Patrick's intention. He always knew that if Evan assumed charge that he'd find some way to cut Brody out, to use any profit for his own means. It's what he's doing now. He's systematically bleeding the company dry. There'll be nothing left in a few months time. Nothing." Helena dug into her handbag and withdrew a typed sheet of paper. "It's why Patrick left specific instructions on his death to give you this."

She watched as Mason's eyes flew over the letter she'd been given by Patrick's lawyer after the will had been read.

"Anyone could've typed this. Even you. Why would he have wanted me to run Davies Freight?"

Helena watched as Mason discarded the letter to let it flutter onto the coffee table.

"I didn't make it up, you have to believe me. Patrick never expected to die so suddenly. He was fit, he was healthy—he expected to live for years more. To have the opportunity to start to groom Brody to take over from him in the future, the way he'd hoped you would until you set up your own firm. But you know how cautious he was. He wouldn't have asked you to do this if he hadn't thought it was important.

"You have to believe me. Evan's after blood. You know he's always been jealous of his father's relationship with me and with Brody. He wants to hurt us."

"Hurt you? C'mon, Helena. I think you're overstating things. Besides, wouldn't it be easier if you just stayed on Evan's side? It's the way people like you operate, isn't it?"

Helena ignored the hurtful inference in Mason's words. As difficult as it was, she had to school herself to be immune to his jibes, no matter how far they were from the truth. She sighed. "You don't know Evan like I do."

"And of course you know him *exceptionally* well, don't you."

Oh no, now he'd definitely gone too far. She leaped from her seat and met him face-to-face, shaking with anger. "Don't you dare suggest that! I would never... I could never..."

"Never?" Mason didn't move so much as a muscle, his voice low and filled with disgust. "You slept with me the night before you pledged yourself to a much older man. A man who could never keep pace with your physical needs. Why wouldn't you turn to someone else? Especially someone who stood to inherit equally with your own son."

"No! I loved Patrick. He became the hub of my whole world. I know I did wrong that night. But I wasn't the only one to blame. I didn't act responsibly, that's true, but I never heard you cry 'stop'. You can't possibly still hold that night against me."

"Can't I? I wasn't the one getting married the next day."

Tears burned in the back of her eyes but she wouldn't give in to them. Too much was at stake. Besides, he was wrong. Despite what she'd thought when she'd entered into her marriage she had loved Patrick. If she could have him back in a minute she would. She owed it to him—for everything he'd done for her, for the wonderful man he'd been—she had to get Mason to agree to help and somehow do it without giving Evan the chance to spread his malicious story and destroy her son's remaining security. She had to appeal to Mason some other way. Patrick must have known how he'd react. In his letter to her he'd been insistent she tell Mason the truth. But at what cost? She drew a steadying breath, deep into her lungs, and turned to face him.

"Please, Mason. Please help. I need your expertise and acumen. You're the only one who can make a difference now. This is Brody's inheritance we're talking about. His whole life lies ahead of him."

"So you're telling me you're not affected by this? You're only doing it for Brody? Your platinum card won't suddenly dry up without that astronomical salary Patrick paid you to decorate a desk at the office? I'm not a fool, Helena. The only person this will make a difference to is you. I'm sure Patrick left Brody more than well provided for."

"Of course. Patrick left both of us well provided for. But you know how much the business meant to him.

From Brody's birth he groomed him to take over one day. You can't simply stand there and let that slip from Brody's future. Besides, this isn't only about Brody and me. Any damage to Davies Freight is going to affect far more people than just me. You have to help."

"Have to? And why is that?"

A painful throb started in her head. She didn't want to do this, but Patrick's instructions had been explicit. She still hadn't even completely gotten over the shock of his letter herself, or the fact that he'd kept the truth hidden from her for so long. That he had, hung heavy in her heart. Gathering all her strength to her, Helena reached out and grasped Mason's forearm in a tight grip.

"Isn't it enough that Patrick asked for your help?"

He flung her a look of absolute distaste. "Through you? No. It's not. I think you overestimate your appeal."

Helena's fingers tightened as she hauled out the courage to say what needed to be said. "Then do it because Brody's your son."

Two

Your son. Your son.

The words echoed in his head, drowning out the roaring denial that filled his brain. Somewhere, deep inside, an intangible flicker leaped at the possibility, but then the heated brand of her fingers fought through the fog of shock to remind him she was there. A part of this—potentially a part of him through Brody—and he didn't trust her. Not so much as a millimetre.

She'd dealt with her grief in record time—it made sense she was on the lookout for her next cash cow, of course she'd look to pin something as outrageous as this on him. There was no way on this wide earth he was going to fall for that one—he'd seen firsthand how destructive a lie like that could be. He placed his hand over hers, peeled her fingers off his arm and dropped her hand.

"I don't believe you." He pitched his voice low and hard so she'd be in no doubt that he could be dissuaded.

She started and paled, as if he'd slapped her.

"You don't…?"

"You've wasted enough of my time, Helena. Now get out of my house." He banked down the anger. He simply wanted her to take her lies and her sexy body somewhere he'd never have to hear them, or see her, again. He stalked across the room, snapped up the handset of a cordless phone and began punching in a series of numbers. "You can wait in the front porch for the taxi."

"No."

His finger hovered over the last digit. "No?"

"I'm not going until you agree to help."

Fury clenched low in his belly like a tight fist. If he had to take her physically from the property himself he'd damn well do it. He dropped the phone back on the side table he'd snatched it from and began to walk toward her, his intent obvious in every step.

"I have proof that Patrick isn't Brody's father."

Mason stopped in his tracks. "Proof?"

"On his death he instructed his solicitor to make certain documents available to me, documents that prove he was incapable of fathering a child."

Mason choked out a humourless laugh and raised one brow. "And Evan? How do you explain him?"

"Adopted."

Sure he was. Was there no end to her lies? "Does he know?"

"Yes. I think that's partly why he's so bitter toward Brody. He thinks Brody is Patrick's natural-born son."

"And you, of course, know he's not."

"I do now."

"Why the hell should I believe you?"

She scrabbled in her bag, withdrew a letter-size envelope and handed it toward him. "Here. Read it yourself."

Reluctantly he took the envelope from her and lifted the flap to remove the folded sheets from within. He sat down on the long sofa facing her chair and began to read.

"So, this proves Patrick was infertile." He tossed the papers back across the coffee table toward her. "It certainly doesn't prove I'm Brody's father. How many other men have you slept with, or are none of them rich enough to pin this onto?"

"Brody is your son. You and Patrick were the only ones."

"You can't possibly expect me to believe that. You might have lost track of the details during your parade of lovers but I remember that night very, very clearly. You were no innocent virgin, Helena."

"Okay, you weren't my first, no, but there was no one else once I married Patrick."

He could neither help, nor wanted to prevent, the incredulous snort that escaped him. He'd been an unwilling audience to Evan's drunken boasts about how athletic his father's beautiful young wife was in bed. He knew she was lying right down to the delicately formed bones of her exquisite body.

A sudden flash of lightning split through the room, rapidly followed by a deafening rumble of thunder and an almighty crash outside. The lights overhead flickered, dimmed and brightened.

He had to get rid of her before the power went out altogether. Mason picked the phone back up and hit the

Talk button. Silence. He hit the button two times in quick succession. Still nothing.

"Problem?" Helena sat back on the chair and crossed her legs.

"Phone's out."

"So use your mobile."

"Can't. This is a black spot. No reception. I'll take you into Whitianga myself. You can check into a motel and get a taxi back home in the morning."

Helena watched in dismay as he grabbed a set of car keys from a softly glazed pottery dish on top of the dining table. That he meant what he said, she had no doubt. Reluctantly she picked up the papers from the table, pushed them back into her bag and rose to follow him through to the garage. If need be she'd come back tomorrow, and the day after that and the day after that until he'd agree to help.

Inside the garage, Mason flipped a switch on the wall. The ceiling light bathed a black behemoth parked in solitary splendour in the middle of the parking bay. She stared at the four-by-four, recognising in its strong powerful lines the personality of the man who drove it— yet, with the chrome running boards and highly polished mag wheels, enough of the daredevil showman who'd brazenly taken the freight community by storm to build the largest privately owned company in the country. The blip of the car alarm disengaging startled her as it echoed in the large area.

"Get in." Mason walked around the other side of the four-by-four, opened the driver's door and climbed up.

With as much dignity as she could muster, Helena opened her door and placed a foot on the running board to give her a lever up into the high leather seat. As she settled in and clipped her seat belt he put the key in the ignition and pressed a button on a remote on the central console. The wooden segmented door behind them slowly lifted open.

A long low-pitched string of expletives ran from Mason's mouth as he looked through the rearview mirror to the driveway. Before she knew what was happening he was out of the truck. What? She unclicked her belt and scrambled back down. Mason stood, just inside the doorway, hands on hips and with frustration and anger roiling off him in tangible waves.

She looked past him and out onto the softly lit forecourt. There, firmly planted across the drive, its tip entangled in dark wires, lay the solid trunk of a toppled pine tree.

"Is that what took the phone out?" Helena looked at the sorry excuse for a tree. It looked as if it should have come down years ago.

"Yeah, it was tagged for removal next week along with a few others. Stay here," he commanded.

"Is there anything—"

"Just do as I said."

Without another word, Mason went to a large storage cupboard along the back wall of the garage and flung open the door. He reached inside and pulled out a set of earmuffs, safety glasses and gloves and a mean-looking chain saw. Setting the saw onto the concrete floor he checked the petrol level, put on the earmuffs, then hefted the saw up again. For a split second, as he passed her, he met her gaze—accusation stark in his angry stare— before striding out into the driving rain. As if it were her fault the stupid tree had come down. Helena crossed her arms defensively in front of her body and fought back a shiver of cold. The temperature had dropped markedly with the onset of the storm.

In a half a dozen steps the driving rain had plastered his shirt to his body. She tried to tear her eyes away from him, from the outline of a supremely well-honed male, but failed miserably. About as miserably as she'd managed to convince him of the truth of Brody's parentage. It *was* her fault. If she hadn't come he wouldn't be out there right now. But she'd had to try—still had to. There was simply far too much at stake.

She should be helping him—after all, he wanted to get rid of her, didn't he? Another gust of wind whipped a flurry of needles and small branches to lash against him as he pulled on the gloves and started up the saw, immediately setting to work to remove the branch nearest him. Before she knew it she was out the door.

"Let me help," she shouted over the ragged noise.

Mason lifted one side of the silencers protecting his ears. "Don't be stupid, it's too dangerous. I told you to stay inside."

She ignored him and gripped a hold of the branch he'd just cut, and dragged it away to the side of the drive.

"Go to the garage and get yourself a set of earmuffs and safety glasses, you'll need them. And Helena?"

She paused and straightened.

"Don't get in my way." The words were nothing but a growl.

She gave a sharp nod to acknowledge his warning. Sure, she wouldn't get in his way, at least not while he wielded that chain saw with the dexterity of a seasoned professional.

From the garage cupboard she pulled out a pair of gardening gloves, although after trying them on she decided to do without. The way they fell off her hands would be more hindrance than help and right now it was more important to her to leave a better impression on Mason than that she'd arrived with.

The rain had soaked through her hair and ran in rivulets beneath the collar of her jacket, sending trickling shivers of discomfort down her spine. She mentally squared her shoulders and focussed on what she had to do. She slipped on the glasses and earmuffs and went back outside.

It was more difficult than she'd expected to clear the branches off to the side, especially in a suit and shoes better suited to a cocktail party than a logging operation.

Mason's eyes burned a hole through her back more than once as she staggered with another branch across the driveway. Through the earmuffs the softened roar of the saw bounced between the bank and the side of the house until Helena's head felt as if it was vibrating in unison with the noise. She pressed fingers, sticky with pine resin, over her earmuffs to seal off any gaps as Mason battled a particularly knotted piece of wood. He wielded the chain saw as if it was second nature to him, but then that's pretty much the way she'd noticed he managed everything in his life. A total perfectionist in whatever he did.

Any other day of the week Helena would have turned tail and left. The discomfort, the noise and the incessant rain would individually have been enough to persuade her to find sanctuary elsewhere. But she couldn't stop. She had to prove she was worth listening to and not, as Mason so clearly thought, just some grasping bimbo out to find her next sugar daddy. She bent to pick up the branch he'd finally worked free and jumped when Mason leaned forward and pulled one of the earmuffs away from the side of her head.

"Ready to give up yet?"

She looked up, raking his face for any clue that she'd satisfied him she wasn't just some pretty thing looking for an easy ride, but his features remained unreadable except for the flicker of heat in his eyes when they dropped to the gaping neckline of her jacket.

"Are you finished yet?" she countered, not daring to move.

Slowly, his eyes trailed back up to her face. "Not yet." His pupils dilated slightly.

Helena felt a brief surge of power. He might act as if he hated her, but he wasn't unaffected by her. At least not as much as he tried to portray. That telltale flare in his eyes had given her more control than she'd dreamed. "Well, then, I'm not finished either."

Despite all the activity, the cold evening air and her wet clothes combined to send a deep chill into her bones. She shivered as she bent to pick up one of the slices of the trunk. Mason reached out to stop her.

"What?" She stood up and put her hands on her hips.

"Go inside, you're wet through."

"It's okay, I can manage," she replied through gritted teeth, bending at the knees to get closer to the richly scented disk of wood.

Mason stood and watched her as she hefted up the piece. Holding it close to her body, she lurched over to where she'd stacked the cut branches. Then, he set to finishing off the remainder of the tree, although she noticed that he cut the slices narrower to make her job a little easier. Eventually he was done and, scooping up three disks to her miserable one each time, they finished clearing the driveway.

"What about that bit?" Helena gestured toward the

tip of the tree that had tangled in and brought down the phone line.

"I'll leave that for the phone guys. C'mon." He gestured toward the garage.

Helena hesitated a moment in the rain, which hadn't let up even the tiniest bit as they'd worked to clear the tree, then followed him back inside. She fought to combat the shivers that now cascaded through her body. The last time she'd come close to feeling this cold she'd been with him, too. Only then the outcome had been vastly different to today. She resolutely pushed away the memory of that night, of the lover who was as far removed from this aloof creature as a person could be.

From beside the passenger door of the truck she watched as he grabbed a rag from the cupboard to wipe down the chain saw and put everything away. She lifted a foot to the running board to climb back into the vehicle when warm hands slipped around her waist and lifted her back down. He only touched her for a moment yet it was enough to send a fire coursing through her body, radiating out from where his hands had rested against her sodden clothing. Fire blended with a bit of something else—something she couldn't afford to acknowledge or identify.

"Forget the road trip tonight."

"You mean it?" Relief coursed through her. The prospect of sitting in cold wet clothing even for the relatively short trip to Whitianga was anathema to her.

"I don't say what I don't mean. Clearing this mess took longer than I expected and we're both soaked through. By the time we get dried out it'll be too late for you to check in anywhere around here. I'll get you some dry things. You can stay in one of the guest rooms."

He sounded as though he'd rather endure a root canal without anaesthetic. Even so, Helena tried to say thank-you but he was already walking away from her. She followed him down the native-timber parquet floor hall to a separate wing of the house that she hadn't noticed on her arrival. He flung open a door at the end of the passage and walked through to another door that led into a large champagne-coloured marble bathroom and snapped on the faucet in the shower. Steam slowly started to fill the room.

"Don't lock the door," he said as he left her. "I'll find something for you to wear and drop it inside."

Helena could barely respond. The lure of warm running water called to her from the shower stall. With cold, stiffened fingers she tried to undo the buttons on the front of her jacket but they just wouldn't cooperate.

"Here, let me."

Warm hands brushed her fingers aside. She shivered as Mason deftly undid the buttons and peeled the tailored jacket from her body. Underneath, her simple black silk camisole clung to her skin, shamelessly exposing the fact she wore no bra. Under his gaze her nipples hardened and pressed against the dark silk. A flush of embarrassment flooded her cheeks.

"I'll be all right from here," she protested as he started to lift the hem of her camisole.

"You're so frozen you can barely move. Be sensible, Helena. Besides, it's not like I haven't seen you naked before."

His fingers brushed against her belly as he took hold of the bottom edge of her cami. The shiver that rippled through her body had nothing to do with cold—his touch scorched like a brand.

"Please, stop." Helena pushed his hands away and stepped backward. "I'll be fine from here. Truly." Blindly, she reached for a towel and pulled it in front of her.

"Whatever you say." He took a step back. "Come through to the living room when you're finished. I'll get the fire going and warm up something for us to eat."

Helena nodded and watched as he left the bathroom. She let go of the breath she'd been holding and swiftly shimmied out of her skirt and peeled off her clinging wet pantyhose and undies. She released her hair from the army of clips that bound it then gratefully stepped beneath the cascade of warmth thundering in the shower. Sheer bliss. She quickly lathered herself up and rinsed off. The stinging needles of the spray invigorated her and although her fingers and toes still felt cold she felt much better. Hungry though. She towelled off her wet skin, and arranged her damp clothes on the heated towel rail to dry, then picked through the mixed assortment of clothing Mason had dumped just inside the door while she'd been luxuriating in the hot water.

In amongst a couple of well-washed soft T-shirts and a pair of grey track pants her hand hesitated over a powder-blue merino wool sweater and a relatively new pair of woman's jeans. Was he sending her a message by including some other woman's forgotten clothing? Resolutely Helena selected a large faded sweatshirt and the track pants. There was no way she would wear another woman's castoffs—years of hand-me-downs from her parents' neighbours combined with the smart remarks from her classmates when she'd worn their old clothing to school had seen to that.

The sudden lance of jealousy that shafted her sideways at the thought of Mason with another woman came as an unpleasant surprise. It's not as if she had any say in his love life, she groaned inwardly, don't even think about it. She'd been a happily married woman herself for twelve years, so why did it suddenly bother her so much to think of another woman's clothing being left here?

With a determined push she shoved the blue sweater under the pile of remaining clothes and dragged on the pants and sweatshirt. The pants were far too large, but they were warm, and she wasn't beyond sacrificing a bit of dignity for warmth right now. She rolled over the waistband several times to try and pull them up a bit on her hips and turned up the legs. The sweatshirt hung almost to the top of her thighs. Well, she decided, looking in the large vanity mirror, she wouldn't win any fashion parades but then she wasn't here to impress anyone, was she. Lord, but her hair was a mess. She rummaged through the vanity drawers, searching for a comb or a brush. Her cheeks flamed as her hand brushed against an unopened twelve-pack of condoms.

"You okay in there?" Mason's voice at the door made her slam the drawer shut. Okay, she could go with the wild look for her hair for now.

Helena opened the bathroom door. "Yes, I'm fine. Thanks for the clothes."

He looked at what she was wearing and then the pile of clothes she'd dumped onto the vanity. If she wasn't mistaken the corners of his mouth lifted slightly for just a moment. She bit her teeth together to avoid verbalising the snaky comment that came unbidden from the jealousy that still twinged inside. He was letting her stay the night. There was no way she was going to do anything to jeopardise his reluctant goodwill.

"Come and eat then."

She followed him back down the hall to the sitting room where the aroma of warmed bread made her mouth water. Fire licked hungrily over split logs in the large stone fireplace and Helena bent to warm her fingers.

"Still cold?" Mason asked.

"Just a bit." Helena grimaced at the state of her fingernails and her hands. No sign now of the elegant manicure she'd had earlier in the week. But it was worth it to get this opportunity. If she hadn't already lugged so much of the tree from one place to another she probably would've hugged it for falling as it did and giving her the chance to stay longer.

"You'll feel better when you've had something to eat. Sit down."

When she was settled in the chair nearest the fire, Mason brought a tray with a bowl of a soup, filled with chunks of vegetables and meat, and several slices of warm French bread. They consumed their meal in silence. It was only as Helena placed her spoon back down in her now-empty bowl that he spoke.

"Thanks for your help outside."

"You're welcome. I don't like standing around while others do all the work."

Mason shot her a look of disbelief. Yeah, she knew what he was thinking. She was no better than a pampered poodle in his eyes. The truth couldn't have been further from his opinion. She knew all about the hard yards and what people had to do to make ends meet. Wealth and privilege hadn't always been tattooed on her forehead. And wasn't that what had put her in this situation in the first place?

Three

Helena held his gaze, defying him to contradict her statement. As their eyes locked in a silent duel, his pupils enlarged, the blackness all but consuming the darker brown iris. The only sound was that of the occasional hiss from the wood in the fireplace as flames consumed the logs and added to the heat escalating in the room. She could feel the throb of her pulse at her neck, and the answering beat from deep inside her. The beat that built in rhythm and send a curl of need to spiral outward from her core.

He hadn't spoken a word, yet in that look—no matter how much he abhorred her—she knew he still wanted her. And she wanted him back. Nothing had changed. The twelve years that lay between them yawned like a chasm—her marriage, their son. Each of them barriers to the desire that clawed with growing hunger and demanded to be assuaged. A log snapped in the fireplace, the sound giving her the impetus she needed to break the stare between them.

She gripped the sides of her tray and stood, making her way quickly to the kitchen. A small groan of discomfort escaped her as her muscles protested their sudden inactivity after the work she'd done outside.

"A bit too much action for you, Helena?"

To anyone else his enquiry would have sounded like no more than a tease, yet in the velvet stroke of his deep voice Helena could only hear contempt.

"Perhaps it's been a bit longer since you actually did 'the work' than you realised?" He deliberately baited her with her own words, twisting them to make her sound foolish.

"Perhaps you're right," she answered softly before moving over to the kitchen where she unloaded her tray and rinsed her dishes in the sink. "Being a good wife involves a different muscle group altogether."

The words had no sooner left her mouth before she regretted them. They were far too easily misconstrued, and in Mason's current frame of mind he would definitely have drawn the wrong impression. His next words only confirmed her fears.

"I can only imagine what you're referring to."

His voice came from right behind her, as steely and cold as a stiletto blade. Helena rotated her shoulders and took a deep breath. It wouldn't matter what she said right now, he wouldn't believe her. He was determined to think the worst.

"Not what you're thinking."

"Whatever you say, Helena. But then you have a habit of leaving out the important details, don't you.

Like being engaged to be married the day after you seduced a total stranger?"

"Mason—"

"Forget it. I don't want to trawl through the past. You made your bed, now you get to reap the consequences. I've been thinking about Brody. You say he's my son."

"He *is* your son."

"I want proof."

"I've shown you—"

"No." Mason crossed his arms in front of him. The black wool of his sweater stretched tight across his shoulders and over his upper arms. Her mouth dried at the latent power he projected, at the superbly sculpted masculine form that lay beneath the finely woven fabric. "Before I'll even consider another step, I want scientific proof."

"A paternity test?"

"Yes."

"And then you'll help us?" She clenched her fingers into fists, her broken nails pressing jagged lines into the palms of her hands. He had to agree.

"If you're telling the truth I'll look into what I can do."

"How soon can we get it done? Where?"

"That's what you'll have to find out when you get back to Auckland, won't you. And quickly, Helena. This had better not drag out any longer than absolutely necessary."

"I'll do whatever I have to, to prove it, Mason. You can count on it."

"Why doesn't that surprise me?" He arched a cynical dark brow and leaned forward, trapping her against the kitchen bench with one hand locked on either side of her hips. "Just get one thing straight in your mind. If I am Brody's father, that doesn't mean I agree to support *you* in any way. Not a cent. Do you understand me?"

Helena sucked in a breath, her nostrils flaring as she inhaled the scent of his woody cologne. To her shame she felt her breasts swell and lift, her nipples tighten and press seekingly against the cotton of her borrowed sweatshirt. Desire pooled low in her belly. "I don't need or want your money, but Brody needs a future. I'll do whatever it takes to satisfy your demands if it means my son's security. Whatever. Do *you* understand *me?*"

"Oh yeah, you're coming through loud and clear." He leaned a little closer. So close she could see the tiny rings of gold around the pupils of his eyes. "Maybe we should start that satisfaction right now."

"Wha—?"

He closed the distance between them. Every nerve in her body fired into attention and Helena felt the air shift as he brought his face to hers. She had a fleeting impression of darkness and heat before his lips were on hard on hers, consuming the startled cry that fled her mouth. She squeezed her eyes closed. She didn't want to think anymore. She didn't want to feel. But despite her wants, her body took on a life of its own, greeting Mason's plunder of her lips with a liquid heat that melted every last bastion of reserve.

His mouth pulled at hers, tasting, sucking, caressing her lips until they were sensitive and swollen. Suddenly she was kissing him back with a hunger she'd thought she'd never experience again. Mason's tongue probed between her lips, invading, taking possession. She met him on his own terms, deepening the kiss, permitting his invasion.

She was lost and helpless against the capacity of emotion that swelled within her. The rational part of her mind ratified his need to dominate her with the power of his passion, but as a tiny moan of desire rose from her throat, Helena admitted she had never wanted a man as much she wanted Mason Knight. She'd suppressed that need, had wrapped herself up in her husband and her son with an intensity that belied her behaviour during that one night she'd spent with Mason. Yet deep inside lurked a craving that hadn't diminished one bit in the past twelve years.

She knew what he thought of her, even understood it in a way. He would hate it that he betrayed his own desire for her in the tiny tremors that rocked his body, in the weight of the insistent erection that pressed against her. Helena lifted her hands with every good intention of shoving him from her, but instead her fingers assumed a life of their own as they dug into his shoulders, relishing the leashed strength of him.

Mason's lips broke away from hers. His breathing came in harshly drawn gasps as he rested his forehead against hers. His eyes were shut, and another shudder rippled through his body. Then, slowly, he pulled back and opened his eyes.

"You're a little rusty," he said in a voice that grated against her ears in scorn. "But it's a start."

A start? She stood, locked in shocked silence as he walked away. In the distance, down the hall, she heard a door swing open then click firmly shut. Then, nothing. Her mind whirled. Was he serious? Did he expect her to become his mistress? When she'd talked about his demands she'd meant for information and for proof of Brody's paternity—but not this, never this. She lifted a shaking hand to her face, her fingers pressing against her swollen lips. She could still feel him there; feel the impression of his body where he'd pressed against hers.

"No," she whispered. "Not again."

Pushing all thoughts of Mason Knight to the back of her mind, Helena automatically went through the motions of clearing up the kitchen and stacking the dishwasher. A minimum of investigation showed her where to store the trays and before long the kitchen was returned to its earlier pristine state. Unfortunately she couldn't say the same for her state of mind. No matter how hard she tried she couldn't get that kiss out of her head. She needed to talk this out with Mason, sort out what his expectations were and make her position quite clear. She'd be no man's plaything. She'd seen and heard more than enough in the past to know she'd rather walk over hot coals than debase herself like that again.

Her mind made up, she stalked down the hallway. Which room was his? A bar of light shone from beneath one of the doors and before she could change her mind Helena rapped sharply on the door and reached to twist the handle.

Mason heard her knock and schooled himself not to spin around at the sound of the door being opened. So, she'd come to him. Somehow, that didn't surprise him. He focussed on the dark vista across the bay, silvered by rain and moonlight, and drew in a deep breath before he turned to face her. A slew of emotions flitted across Helena's face. First, something akin to anger and determination, but it was closely followed by a hesitance that assured him—despite how his body had flamed to life only minutes ago, and still smouldered—he continued to hold the upper hand.

"What did you mean by that comment?" While the words were a demand, he observed, the delivery was sadly lacking. A telltale tremor in her voice confirmed she was still shaken by their kiss. As shaken as he was himself, no doubt, although there was no way she'd ever know that.

"Comment?"

"Don't play word games with me, Mason. You know what I'm talking about." She stared at a spot just to the side of his face, clearly unwilling to make eye contact.

"Why don't you tell me what's bothering you, Helena?" He swiftly crossed the room, coming to a halt to stand directly in front of her and forcing her to look up to meet him eye to eye.

"What you said—a start. A start to what?"

His mouth quirked at one corner. The million-dollar question. He lifted a hand and reached for a long tendril of her hair, rubbing its silky texture between his fingers, taking his time over his response.

"Well now, that all depends on you, Helena. As I recall we were discussing demands and satisfaction. Your demands. My satisfaction."

"Brody's your son. I shouldn't have to make any demands on you."

Mason let go the piece of hair and let his finger drop to the exposed prominence of her collarbone where the neckline of his sweatshirt dipped against her skin. She felt like satin, cool smooth luxurious satin, and held herself rigid as if his touch had frozen her in place. But beneath the fabric he could see what effect he had on her and he could hear the catch in her breathing as he traced a line to the top of her shoulder and round to the nape of her neck.

"Let's not discuss Brody just now. Not until I have the information I require." He slid his hand behind her neck, cupping it with his palm. "I'm curious about what you're prepared to do, Helena. What, exactly, you define as 'whatever it takes.'"

He lifted his other hand to cup her jaw and tilted her head gently upward toward his. His voice dropped an octave. "This, perhaps?"

He bent his head to capture her mouth with his again, to stroke his tongue against the seam of her lips, to draw the full swollen flesh of her lower lip into his mouth and plunder beyond it with a possessive sweep.

"Or maybe this?" He skimmed his hand from the back of her neck down her spine to press her lower body forward, into his, against the aching arousal that demanded to be assuaged.

"No," she whispered against his mouth.

"Be honest with me, Helena. Be honest with yourself." He kissed her again, holding her to him, feeling the taut resistance of her body as he tasted and suckled at her lips and exulting in the moment she surrendered her will to his own—when her body moulded against his as if she'd been carved from his very flesh.

He let go of her jaw and slipped his hand up underneath the waistband of her top to trace his fingers against the texture of her skin, slowly working the material away from her body until his fingers could splay across the warm globe of her breast. He plucked gently at the hardened nub of her nipple, playing the tender flesh until she sagged against his body and groaned deep in her throat.

Barely taking a second to release her lips, he swept the sweatshirt up and over her body. Both his hands spanned her tiny waist and skimmed over her rib cage, his thumbs trailing twin lines under the swell of her breasts.

He watched her face as he touched her; saw the glitter of desire in her eyes before they slid closed. Her parted lips were moist and swollen, an open invitation. He should stop now. He should be repulsed by her eagerness to welcome his touch, his body. Instead, his arousal escalated another notch. He felt her reach for the waistband of her pants, saw as she gripped the fabric with fisted hands then pushed until the sweats fell in a pool at her feet. Total surrender. Total capitulation. She was his to do with as he wished.

Mason swept her small frame up in his arms and placed her gently against the covers on his bed. As he settled over her body he bent to kiss her lips, her cheeks, her eyelids. Helena's arms wrapped around his shoulders, the fingers of one hand splayed against the back of his neck, encouraging him to hasten. To take her lips, to take her body.

But he would not be hurried. Every part of her face, her jaw, her throat, fell victim to the relentless, but painfully tentative, attention he paid her. Attention he'd dreamed of more nights that he could count. Attention that had wound him in knots of frustration for more years than he wanted to remember. He trailed his lips and tongue down her throat, stopping only to nip gently at the edge of her neck. The gasp of pleasure that escaped her spurred him on his path and he bent his head to capture one tightly budded nipple between his lips. His tongue swirled with delicious intent around the hardened peak, drawing it into his mouth and suckling with a steady rhythmic pull. She squirmed against him, silently urging him to press his body harder against hers.

He wore too many clothes. Mason lifted himself and managed to divest himself of his shirt and unbuckle his jeans. He clenched his teeth against the roaring torrent of desire that threatened to swamp him as his body finally settled, skin against skin—as her breasts flattened against the hard planes of his chest. Protection, damn, he needed protection. He dragged himself away from her welcoming body to reach in the bedside cabinet drawer. If he didn't take care of things now it would be too late. Sheathing himself took only a moment but even then the time away from her heat was an eon.

Helena lifted a trembling hand to stroke his face, tracing the outline of his cheekbones, his jaw, committing every touch, every texture to memory. She shouldn't be doing this, but she wanted him with a fiery need she barely recognised in herself. She trailed her fingers over his lips before letting her hand drop to her breast where she repeated the caress across her aching nipples. His pupils dilated at her action, his chest shuddered with uneven breaths. She cupped her breasts with both hands—offering herself to him. Her skin, so sensitive now, it begged for him to touch her again. His eyes blazed over her, watching as she arched her body along the sheets. A primitive beat pounded through her veins, heightening her senses and her awareness of the man who watched her every move with the intentness of a panther stalking its prey. A piercing shaft of anticipation arrowed through her as he covered her body, length for length, driving a small whimper of sheer need to shudder from her lips.

Mason caught her face between his hands—forcing her to meet his gaze, defying her to break the contact. He slid inside her—slowly, completely—filling her with a sense of belonging that both terrified and soothed her. She drew him deeper inside, and took the groan wrenched from his very core as her reward.

He began to move, first slowly then in increasing tempo, fuelling the delicious tension that escalated within her. A fine sheen of perspiration broke out on her skin and her heartbeat accelerated, matching the cadence of their movements. Still, he held her with his eyes—still, she remained trapped. Drawn inexorably to him as if her existence depended on their ephemeral link. Helena gave herself over to the sheer volume of feeling that ebbed and flowed within and around her. Her sight began to glaze, her eyelids to flutter and a deep-throated sigh expelled past her lips as her climax approached. When Mason's hands let her go, she tilted her head back and lifted her hips to take him in as deeply as she could bear. Except suddenly her body was bereft of his heat, empty of his possession.

"No!" she cried. "Not now, please, don't stop now." Helena struggled to push herself up onto her elbows as Mason pulled away from her and got up from the bed.

"What's wrong?" Her voice, thick with desire, hung in the air between them as he watched her impassively. She fought to control her rapid breathing. A shiver rippled over her as the air caressed her flushed skin. Under his cool scrutiny Helena felt reduced to little more than a butterfly on a pin. Something bad had happened, something she didn't understand, and now she desperately wished she could cover her aching naked body from the emptiness in his gaze.

"There's nothing wrong." His answer was delivered at subzero temperature.

"Then why? Why did you stop?"

Mason bent to gather his clothing and yanked his jeans up his long legs and over his hips. "Because I can." He collected the sweatshirt and pants she'd worn earlier and tossed them onto the bed. The inference in his action was clear. Get dressed and get the hell out of his room. "And because now I know how far you're prepared to go."

Helena scrambled to cover her vulnerability, her skin still sensitised to his touch, her body still craving the release he'd denied them both. On trembling legs she sped across the carpet and through the door, the click of the latch behind her almost inaudible against the echo of her fractured breath as the reality drew home with terminal velocity.

Because I can. The words echoed hollowly inside her mind. In three words he'd reduced her to nothing but some *thing* to be enjoyed at his convenience. She'd allowed herself to be degraded to nothing more than what she was essentially fighting so hard to forget. It was as if she'd learned nothing in the past twelve years. Anger lanced through her body, followed swiftly by burning pain that billowed from deep within her chest. Helena pushed a fist against her mouth to hold back the scream that built inside, because she was suddenly frightened that if she let the sound go she'd never be able to stop.

In his bathroom Mason dispensed with the redundant condom—balling it up in tissue and flinging into the wastebasket with a guttural curse. He didn't know what he hated more at this moment—the fact that he'd made love to Helena, or the fact she'd let him. Made love, ha! He'd succumbed to a primal urge, nothing else—and if he kept telling himself that for long enough, he'd even begin to believe it.

He stepped into the shower stall, switched the water to as hot as he could stand and, resting his forehead against the wall, let the water pound against his shoulders.

He'd said no. It had seemed so important at the time

to be able to walk away—to resist her. To be in control. The victory should be pulsing through him, yet all he could feel was the acrid taste of failure compounded by intense clawing need. The compulsion to stamp himself on her body, her psyche, tormented him. Urged him to wipe away every memory she held of every other man— and there had been plenty of them, he was certain.

She'd responded to him so immediately, so intensely. A piece of him wanted to believe that her response had been for him, and him alone, but he knew her type too well. The painfully familiar nausea swelled inside him as he remembered the careful yet inappropriate brush of a hand, the kiss that lingered a little too long on his cheek and then later, in his room one night, the blatant offer from his father's much younger mistress. Yeah, he knew the type all right, and now he knew just how to handle her.

It helped that he had something over her—she needed his help. And then there was Brody. If the boy was his son he'd be doing him a complete favour to remove him from her influence, from the steady stream of men through the revolving door of her bedroom. No wonder she had Brody away at boarding school down country, she didn't have to be accountable for her behaviour this way. But not for much longer if the paternity test results validated her claim. Things were going to change.

Mason reached for the shower mixer and twisted it one-eighty degrees before lifting his face to the stream of water. He flinched as the spray flung cold needles at his body, almost to the point of pain, then snapped off the mixer when his blood had finally cooled to what approximated normality. It was a shame the same couldn't be said for his flesh. Damn her for having this effect on him, and damn him for letting her.

Four

Dawn slanted thick, pink streaks, laden with the threat of rain, across the sky, its light like a probe across her face. Even at her lowest, when she'd done things that had shamed her dreadfully, she hadn't felt this used.

Because I can.

Did he think he was so superior to her, so much stronger that he could use her and then just walk away? Of course he could. He held all the cards in this particular hand and he knew it.

Helena dragged herself from the twisted bed sheets and padded into the bathroom. God, she looked a wreck. She'd ended up going to bed in the tracksuit. Suddenly she couldn't bear to wear it a moment longer. She needed the reminder of his touch against her skin about as much as she needed a garden party right now. She slid out of the clothes—Mason's clothes—and kicked them across the floor. If only getting out of this situation were equally as easy. She plucked her underpants off the heated towel rail and pulled them on, swiftly followed by her camisole and skirt. The waistband of the skirt still felt damp and clammy to her skin, but at least she was wearing her own clothes.

Her clothes. Her decisions.

One way or another she'd deal with her problems, even if it included dealing with Evan. It had been Patrick's wish that she disclose the truth about Brody's parentage to Mason. She'd followed that wish to the letter. Now the ball was in Mason's court. She certainly wasn't going to stick around here and be a victim of his dictates any longer. The sooner she was gone, the sooner she could begin to garner the strength she needed for what she knew would be an arduous battle ahead.

Helena gathered up her handbag and let herself quietly out of the bedroom. The house was silent and still. Too still. She sucked in a deep breath, letting it out slowly to calm her sudden nerves then resolutely made her way down the passage. It wasn't until she'd picked up the cordless phone in the sitting room that she remembered the line was dead. How on earth would she get a taxi now?

There was nothing else for it but to walk down to the main road and hope she could get a ride with some passerby. However, at the front door Helena was stymied once again. Obviously Mason had brought his city habits here to the Coromandel. The front door was locked and a quick reconnoitre of the entranceway proved futile in the search for a key to let herself out the house.

The garage. What about the garage? The automatic garage door opener would have a wall-mounted control as well. She let herself into the garage and carefully closed the door behind her. Only a small amount of light filtered through the high windows in the wooden automatic doors and it took her a while for her eyes to adjust to the gloom in the garage.

The bank of switches by the door had been labelled by some organised soul. Mason, she didn't doubt. She knew he'd done a stint in the army. The way he kept things rigidly organised here at the house was no doubt a follow-on effect to his military training. Helena swiftly identified the switches that operated the garage door and the gate at the bottom of the private road. Her hand hovered over the switches hesitating briefly before depressing them. The garage door slowly opened.

It would be so much easier if she could simply drive out of here. Her stomach lurched uncomfortably as her eyes tracked across the garage to Mason's four-by-four. The beast was way bigger than the small sedan she'd lost to the river twelve years ago. Could she do it? Could she drive again?

She walked across the tiled garage floor and pulled open the driver's door, swinging up into the seat before she could think twice about it. Her hands shook as she laid them on the steering wheel. Fear washed over her in a sickening wave and Helena closed her eyes in a vain attempt to force down the choking nausea that pitched through her.

"You'll need these."

Mason's voice from just outside the open vehicle made her jump. From his fingers dangled a set of car keys. He was dressed all in black again today, the solid darkness lending a lethal edge to his appearance.

"I wasn't…" Her voice trailed off. She had no idea what she was thinking.

"Sure you weren't." He leaned across and inserted one of the silver keys into the ignition. "There you go."

He stood back and crossed his arms, silent challenge visible in his stance and the fierce expression in his eyes. She couldn't move. Couldn't bring herself to turn that key.

"What's stopping you, Helena?"

"I can't…I can't drive anymore." Her voice shook almost as much as her hands, and her stomach twisted.

"You used to."

"That was different. It was a long time ago."

"It's going to be difficult to run away from me if you don't."

She swivelled her head to face him. "I'm not running away. Not from you."

"Of course you're not. So go on. Do it."

There was a thread of steel to his voice, an underlying fury that both frightened and galvanised her into action. Helena reached forward and turned the key, bringing the four-by-four to sudden rumbling life.

"Still remember what comes next?"

Helena flung him a withering look. "Sure I do." She pulled the driver's door closed with a hollow *thunk* and selected Reverse to put the vehicle in motion. Her hands felt clammy on the wheel and her stomach was doing the kind of acrobatics that more appropriately belonged in a Cirque du Soleil performance. She backed out of the garage, spinning the wheel to turn in the parking bay so she could head off in the right direction down the drive. A quick glance in the rearview mirror confirmed Mason still stood in the garage, his arms crossed in front of him, his feet planted firmly on the ground.

She *could* do this. If only to show him.

Helena slipped the transmission into drive and held

her breath as the vehicle jerked forward. Another glance in the rearview mirror showed Mason hadn't moved an inch. She hooked up her seat belt then planted her foot firmly on the accelerator.

The truck fishtailed slightly as she took the sharp corner that turned from the driveway onto the private road that lead down to the main route back to civilization. Helena kept the momentum up, braking gently before she reached a blind bend in the road. Something wasn't right. A sea of mud, littered with small trees and debris, encroached on the unsealed surface. There was no way she could drive through all of that at this speed. She stomped on the brake and pulled the steering wheel sharply to the left.

She knew the exact moment the vehicle lost its grip on the loose metal road and, without losing momentum, felt the precise point at which the front edge of the bull bars connected with the bank, spinning her around, until with a muffled metallic wallop, the entire right side connected with the hard wall of earth that lined the road. The truck groaned as it settled back on its four wheels, rocking slightly in the process. The passenger door flung open.

"Are you okay?" Breathless, Mason climbed in and ran his hands over her chest and shoulders, frantically checking her for injuries.

"I… I don't think I'm hurt," Helena managed in a shaky voice as tremors shuddered through her.

"It's my fault. I shouldn't have pushed you."

"No. It's me. I chose to do it. I should've known better. I shouldn't have let you goad me into it." Helena felt her eyes flood with tears, felt the hot liquid spill over her lashes and track down her cheeks.

Strong arms wrapped around her shoulders and pulled her into the warm haven of Mason's body.

"Are you sure you're okay?" His broad hands cradled her head and gently ran through her hair, testing her scalp for any tenderness. He tilted her face toward his. "When I heard the crash I…" Mason shook his head, as if to dislodge the sharp lines of concern etched into his pale face. His thumbs reached up and brushed away the tears that rolled down her face.

"Don't cry, babe." His voice was strange, tight.

Helena felt the air shift between them as he brought his face to hers. His lips, when they touched, were hot, consuming. She softened against him, squeezing her eyes closed against the stark need she saw reflected in his gaze. She didn't want to think anymore. She didn't want to feel. But despite her wants, her body took on a life of its own, greeting Mason's possession of her lips with an answering flare of heat that melted every nerve ending. His mouth slanted across hers and she welcomed the power in his kiss. Tremors rocked his body like tiny after-shocks.

She wondered fleetingly if perhaps they were not all triggered by desire, but out of relief she hadn't been hurt—that somewhere inside he actually cared that she was okay. But as a tiny moan of desire rose from her throat, Helena knew she'd never be okay again. Not as long as she remained in Mason's arms. Not as long as she allowed him to feed the fire of her need for him— a need she'd denied for the last twelve years. A need ignited by a chance encounter a lifetime ago. She thought she'd learned to live without it, without wanting him. It hadn't been easy, but she'd made her choice and stood by it.

Mason lifted his head, resting his forehead briefly against hers before letting her go from his embrace. Without another word, he got out of the vehicle and stalked around to the front of the four-by-four. Helena watched in silence as anger, then resignation, flew across his face at the sight of the damage to the side of the truck.

"Pop the hood," he called in a clipped tone.

With a trembling hand Helena reached under the dash to find the necessary lever. She sighed in relief when she found the right one and the hood was raised as a visual barrier between them. She touched her fingers to her lips. Lord help her, would the wanting never go away?

Mason slammed the hood down with a heavy thud. He shouldn't have done it. He shouldn't have goaded her into driving when she was obviously not ready for it. By the same token, he knew she shouldn't have attempted to drive, especially something as powerful as what his brothers teasingly referred to as "the Black Beast." He could shake her for taking such a risk.

His gut clenched when he thought again of how badly she could have been hurt. The visual image that had imprinted across his mind when he'd heard the impact, of Helena's broken and bleeding body trapped in his wrecked truck, flared vividly. He shook his head and blinked hard to dismiss the all too graphic picture and took a deep breath. For reasons he didn't want to dissect, the thought of Helena coming to harm had frightened him so much that he'd flown down the drive like a 200-metre sprint champion. The relief that she'd been okay had been sharp, coming from deep inside.

He welcomed the anger that now followed— embraced it, as it gave him the opportunity not to examine his feelings too closely. Instead, it allowed him to focus on the physical damage to his truck and brought him some much needed composure. He was familiar with the cold tang of fury on his tongue when he thought of Helena. It was quantifiable. Justified. Worrying about her was not. Satisfied he'd reassumed control, he leaned back in through the passenger door.

"Hop out. I'll see if we can get the truck back to the house. I need to check if it can still make the trip back to Auckland." Mason extended a hand to help Helena climb across the front seats. He gritted his teeth when she rejected his overture of assistance. Fine, she wanted to manage without his help, so be it. Let's just see how long that would last.

He stood aside while Helena clambered gingerly over the seats. She was still as white as a ghost; her green eyes bright as emeralds in her pale face. His hands itched to draw her to him, to reassure himself once more that she was okay, but he suppressed the urge, focusing instead on the desire to give her a good shaking, which hadn't completely deserted him.

Nor had the desire to kiss her again. He was going to have to either get that out of his system soon, or learn to come to terms with it. And if the past was any indicator, he wasn't going to come to terms with it soon. He had to remind himself sharply of the reason why she'd invaded his haven.

Cursing under his breath, Mason climbed into the cab and settled behind the steering wheel. He turned the key in the ignition and heaved a massive sigh of relief when the engine turned over the first time. He eased the truck into gear and slowly drove forward, pulling away from the bank as he did so.

The scraping sounds against the side of his once highly polished paintwork was enough to bring tears to a grown man's eyes. Away from the bank, Mason slipped the truck into neutral and, leaving it idling, shoved and pushed against the driver's door until it could open enough for him to get out.

"Ah, hell." Mason shook his head again. Bare metal, crumpled and scratched panels. She'd made a fine mess. One of the wheel guards had buckled in and rubbed against the tyre. Knowing he needed to do something physical to relieve his suppressed anger and frustration—before it reached volcanic proportions—he burned up excess energy dragging the reluctant metal away from the rubber. The physical damage done to the truck could be repaired, but it wasn't going to be as easy to ignore the fire that still licked heatedly through his veins.

"Get in."

She flinched at his sharply bitten command, but at this precise moment he wasn't concerned with her mental fragility. The steam coming out from under the hood was beginning to tell its own story. The four-by-four would never make the trip back to Auckland and there was no way he was spending another night with her under his roof. He'd have to arrange alternative transport, and quickly.

Once she was settled he coaxed the vehicle back up the road and parked it in the garage.

"I need to climb up the hill, see if I can get a cell phone signal so I can make some calls. Why don't you make us some coffee." He gestured toward the kitchen, and was relieved when she gave a small nod.

Some time later, the aroma of freshly-brewed coffee tantalised his nostrils as he walked back to the sitting room. As he entered, Helena poured a mug of coffee and handed it to him.

"I'm sorry for what I did to the truck." She shook her head, not meeting his eyes. "After last night, I…"

A pang of remorse prodded Mason's conscience but it was short-lived. She'd come here without his permission. He couldn't afford any sympathy for a woman who'd barter her child—potentially *his* child—to preserve her lifestyle. What was it she'd said again? Oh yeah, *I'll do whatever it takes to satisfy your demands.* Last night had shown him just how far she was prepared to go. A curl of tension started low in his belly. No matter how hard he tried he could not remain immune to her. It was something he was going to have to handle. Last night had only whetted his appetite for more. Leaving her, as he'd done, had drawn its own satisfaction—and its own torment.

"Forget last night. The helicopter will be at the pad soon. Drink your coffee."

In confirmation of his words, the distant beat of rotor blades in the air approached the house.

"Helicopter?"

"It's the quickest way to get back to Auckland. Do you have a problem with that?" He downed his coffee in one quick gulp.

"No. No problem."

"Good. The sooner we get back the sooner you can find out when we can get the paternity test done."

"How am I going to do that without Brody finding out what it's for? I've been thinking about it and I don't want him to know that Patrick wasn't his father. He's been through enough already."

Mason bit back the retort that sprang to mind.

Typical. She wanted it all—his help with Brody and with Davies Freight, but no acknowledgement if her paternity claim proved to be correct. Why didn't that surprise him?

"We'll cross that bridge when the results come in. With respect to the testing, I'm sure you can use your imagination to find something that won't rouse his suspicions."

"He's a clever boy, Mason. He'll ask questions."

"Then you'll just have to be one step ahead, won't you. Get this clear in your head, Helena. Without proof, I'm not lifting a finger to help you. With that incentive you're bound to come up with something."

Five

The sound of the chopper overhead put an end to any further desire to battle the situation out with her.

"Come on." Mason led the way out of the house, snatching up his briefcase in the front entrance on the way. Beside the garage a path was cut in the bank, leading up to where a sleek black chopper, emblazoned with Black Knight Transport in gold along the side, had settled on the designated landing pad.

The pilot stepped down from the craft, opening the side door to usher Helena into a luxurious passenger compartment before ducking around the back to climb in on the other side of the cockpit. Mason secured his briefcase then settled himself in the pilot's seat.

Helena sat in the back, alone and feeling like a pariah. The journey back to Auckland could only have taken about thirty minutes, but it felt like forever, seated as she

was in splendid isolation. By the time the chopper set
down at Ardmore Airfield her stomach had tied in knots.
Mason opened the door to help her alight but, as before,
she refused his assistance. It was all very well that he ex-
hibited such gentlemanly manners, but it was more than
she could bear to let her fingers linger in his hand—to
feel the hard, dry warmth of his fingers and not remember
how they'd felt as they'd driven the wild response from
her body last night. How he'd rejected her.

"Thank you," she managed through stiff lips. "I'll
call a cab to get home from here."

"A cab? I don't think so. I'll see you get home."

"A cab was good enough for me last night," she
reminded him tartly.

"I didn't believe I had a potential vested interest in
you then. Like I said, I'll see you home."

She bristled at his overbearing response but ac-
quiesced silently. What else could she do? She was
between a rock and a hard place, either at his mercy or
Evan's. She didn't know which was worse.

A shiny black late-model Porsche stood parked next
to a hangar, a tall, slim young man standing by it. Mason
walked toward it, lifting his hand to catch the keys the
younger man threw to him with a smile and a word of
thanks. When he noticed she hadn't followed, he
stopped and turned. The look in his eyes left her with
no doubt that if he had to pick her up and insert her body
into the vehicle he'd do it. With a tiny sigh she covered
the distance between them, hoping against hope that the
car could make the journey to her home in as short a
time as its smooth lines suggested. The sooner this
weekend came to an end, the better.

* * *

"What do you want me for, Knight?" Evan Davies stumbled a little as he rose from the chaise longue situated in the hotel lobby where Mason had asked to meet him. "It's Sunday night. I've got better things to do than discuss business with you." His words slurred slightly.

The strong smell of alcohol hit Mason square in the nose, but he bit his tongue. Evan's dissolute features aged him beyond his years. His excessive playboy lifestyle had caught up to him with a vengeance. It was hard to believe they were both the same age.

"I think you'll like what I have to say. Come upstairs. I've reserved a suite for our discussion."

Once in the plush suite, Evan went straight for the whiskey decanter on the sideboard in the main sitting room, pouring a generous serving before sinking into one of the large leather-covered sofas angled to appreciate the sumptuous harbour view.

"So spit it out. I haven't got all night."

"I want to make you an offer for your shares in Davies Freight."

Evan's short bark of laughter cut through the air. "You're kidding me, right? Black Knight Transport wants to merge with Davies Freight? It's a money soak hole. Why the hell would you want to buy it? Your distribution contracts outearn anything Davies Freight could bring you."

The information Mason had gleaned today had proven that the situation with Davies Freight was far worse than he'd imagined. The company was bleeding funds—badly. He had his suspicions about who was responsible. "I have my reasons." Mason remained standing, his fists pushed deep into his trouser pockets.

"One of those reasons wouldn't be about five foot four with come-to-bed green eyes and sexy chestnut hair, would it?" Evan's watery blue eyes narrowed speculatively. "You know she controls Brody's share of the company. Whatever you've got in mind, she's going to have to agree, too. I've tried to get that share off her already. She's not in a cooperative mood. Even telling her that it was our last chance to make some money off of dear old Dad's failing business wasn't enough to get her to sell. What makes you think you'll change her mind?"

"She'll agree." Mason's response was clipped.

Evan got up and refilled his glass, taking a big swig before tilting his head and eyeing Mason carefully. "You sound pretty sure of yourself. I wondered when she'd move on to her next conquest, especially when I disagreed with her about keeping Davies Freight going. Making the widow merry, are we?"

Mason fought the need to bite back at the other man's snide remark—to wipe the self-indulgent *knowing* expression off Evan's face. "What were you thinking of, Evan, offering to buy her out? You know the company is going to the wall anyway."

An expression of sheer hatred crossed the other man's features. "You want to know why? I'll bloody tell you. There's no way her whiney little brat is entitled to what should have been all mine. I want to sell the whole lot, but the stupid bitch won't let go of her baby's entitlement. I had a buyer lined up and everything. Of course he's gone cold on the idea now—he's not interested in half shares."

"I am. State your price."

Evan almost dropped his drink. He bent to put the glass down heavily on the coffee table in front of him.

"You want her that much?" he whistled long and low. "I'm impressed. She's good, but not *that* good, if you know what I mean." He winked and reached for his glass again.

Mason was a step ahead of him and moved the glass across the table, out of reach. "How much?" he demanded.

Evan sat back and announced a figure that would have had Mason laughing for weeks if he wasn't so firmly set on his path. "Done."

"Done? Just like that?"

"Just like that." Mason flipped open his cell phone and made a call. "Yeah, bring the contract up now. He agreed."

Before he'd even hung up Evan's sick laugh filled the room. "Boy, you really have it bad for her, don't you? What's she promised you, hmm? Extras? You know her type gets a lot more for extras. It's how she met dear old Dad, don't you know? Yep, there's a lot more to our darling Helena than meets the eye."

"What the hell are you talking about? They met in Wellington on a business trip."

"Is that what he told you? Yeah, sure. It figures." Evan smiled nastily. "She was an escort. You know the type—the higher you pay 'em, the lower they're prepared to go. Then again, maybe you don't. You've never had to buy the company of a willing woman, have you? Ha! Looks like you have now. I hope she's worth it, but from what I've experienced, I doubt it."

Evan's words fell like acid rain against Mason's skin. He was hard-pressed not to drive his clenched fist into the man's smug features. *An escort.* Suddenly her behaviour all began to make sense. How she'd seduced him that night in the truck. How she'd played the reluctant card on Friday night, yet still found her way into his bed. All along she'd played him with the oldest game in history.

A metallic taste filled his mouth and he realised he was biting the inside of his cheek. Damn her and all women like her. He wasn't falling for that again. Oh, he was sure they'd end up in bed again. There was a magnetic pull from deep inside his gut that drew him to her—no point in denying it. But there was one thing he was certain of—when it did happen it would be totally on his terms. Every step of the way.

The doorbell to the suite rang and Mason crossed over to open the door. His younger brother, Connor, head of the corporate law office for Knight Enterprises—their father's company—and the family's lawyer, stood with a briefcase in his hand, worry clear in his eyes.

"Are you sure about this, Mase? The figures don't look good. It's not a strong move for BKT."

"I know. I have my reasons. C'mon, let's get this over with."

Once the legal necessities were taken care of, Connor left and Mason turned to face Evan.

"Don't ever set foot near Davies Freight or Helena again. Do you understand?"

"Hey, you bought the company, not the dame. She's open to offers."

Mason stepped up to Evan, grabbed his shirt front in his fist, twisting it and drawing his clenched hand up under Evan's chin. He took great care to enunciate each word very clearly so there was no way Evan wouldn't get the message. "Stay away from Helena."

Beads of sweat broke out on Evan's pasty forehead. "Sure, mate. Whatever you say. I've about had enough of her anyway." He stumbled backward and fell onto the sofa as Mason released him.

Mason reached into his pocket and spun the room's key-card through the air. It landed against Evan's paunch. "Keep the suite for the night. It's all paid up. Anything else on the tab is your expense. Don't spend all your money at once."

He turned and stalked to the door. He wasn't spending another second in the same air space as this scumbag. He couldn't wait to be shot of the other guy, couldn't wait to wash the whole experience off his skin and out of his mind. If only getting Helena out of his system would be as easy. The satisfaction that he was now one step ahead of Helena's grasping greed should be overwhelming right now, yet still it remained beyond his reach. Instead, the sour tang of disappointment left a bad taste on his tongue.

By nine o'clock Monday morning Helena had the information she needed to set the paternity testing in motion. She'd spent time on the weekend searching the net and had been relieved to locate New Zealand's sole diagnostic lab for that area of work in Auckland. Armed with the data she took a taxi to work and, on her mental list of jobs for the day, made calling Mason her first priority. She was so preoccupied with her findings she didn't notice the buzz of activity at the ground-floor reception which coordinated the vast freight forwarding enterprise that made up Davies Freight; she missed the slightly frantic wave from Mandy, her receptionist. She flew up the stairs to the next floor, determined to tackle what stood firmly in her mind as her least favourite task to deal with today.

She noted with relief that Patrick's office door was closed as she made her way to her office. Evan must be inside, but the fact he had the door shut meant she needn't face his demands or his filthy double entendres right now—thank goodness. She slipped out of her jacket and hooked it onto the coat hanger behind her office door and sank down into her desk chair, finding comfort in the organised chaos that reigned across her desk and every available surface. Here was where she felt most alive. Most useful.

The business management degree she'd attained through part-time studies after Brody had been born was, next to her son, the thing in her life of which she was most proud. Patrick had insisted she continue with her studies when they'd married, giving her coaching and tips with her assignment work that had seen her graduate in the top ten percent of her class. Attaining her qualification had made everything worthwhile— even what she'd done to survive that awful year when she'd discovered her parents had mortgaged their home to put her through varsity. That in itself wouldn't have been so bad but when her dad lost his job teaching at the small country school where they'd lived due to a Ministry of Education downsizing, she'd been frantic to make the money back for them.

They'd sacrificed their retirement dream to see her enrolled into University without the hassle and financial pressure of a student loan, but the responsibility had lain heavily on her shoulders. When a friend had suggested she sign up at a modelling and escort agency to earn a few dollars, the idea had been a godsend. The money was good and she only worked when she could fit it in around her lectures and exams. Besides, it wasn't as if it was in any way taxing—she'd been no more than a pretty, conversational arm adornment for out-of-town businessmen. Until that last time, when her client decided to breach the terms of his contract with the agency and wouldn't take no for an answer. It had been that one final unpleasant incident that had blessedly led her to Patrick, who'd been staying at the same hotel where her client had made the ugly scene.

Patrick's calm command of the situation had despatched the other man in no uncertain terms and she'd spent the rest of the evening in his company, letting him coax her story from her and accepting his assurance that everything would work out okay.

Tears pricked at her eyes and she reached for the silver-framed family portrait, taken only weeks before his heart attack. He'd kept it in the library at home, the room which had doubled as his office. Since he'd passed away, she'd kept it here on her desk. It made her feel as though he was still there for her somehow. She reached out a finger to trace his features. She had so much to be grateful to Patrick for, and now she'd never be able to let him know.

Lost in her memories, the buzz of her phone startled her.

"Yes, Mandy?"

"Sorry to disturb you, Mrs. Davies, but you're wanted in Mr. Davies' office."

"Thank you, Mandy. Let Evan know I'll be right along."

Helena fought to quell the rising dread in her stomach. Dealing with Evan always made her feel ill. His dislike of her had been cunningly veiled during her marriage to Patrick, but since his father's death he'd been a thorn in her side and had made her life—and Brody's—as difficult as humanly possible. His vicious contempt, coupled with the lascivious way he always looked at her, made her wish she'd worn something with more coverage than the deep V-neck midnight-blue collarless blouse and matching tailored skirt which skimmed her knees.

Oh well, she sighed, there was nothing for it but to face him. The short distance between the offices was covered all too quickly. She hesitated a moment, smoothing her hands over her hair, which fell in a waving chestnut waterfall to her shoulders, and then her clothing to make sure she looked okay before rapping sharply on the door and letting herself in.

"You wanted me?"

"Good of you to turn up this morning. I trust you have a good reason for being so late," a deep well-modulated and all too familiar voice stopped her in her tracks.

Mason! What was he doing here? Her eyes raked the stony-faced self-made tycoon as he sat in his designer suit behind her dead husband's desk. If she'd found him remote—even for a moment—over the weekend, his demeanour now supplanted any such memory. He was as impassive and impenetrable as a Mount Cook face and, judging by the stern set of his mouth, just as dangerous.

"Surprised to see me? Good. This way we can avoid any false expressions of your questionable work ethic."

"There's nothing wrong with my work ethic. You don't even know what I do around here." Helena's spine stiffened in outrage. How dare he turn up at her company office and accuse her of not doing her job? What the heck was he doing here anyway?

"Ah yes, what you do around here. I've gathered some idea." He snapped closed the folder of bank statements he'd been perusing and leaned forward on the desk. "What kept you this morning?"

"I was finding out about the paternity testing—it wasn't something I wanted to do here at work." She crossed her arms in front of her. "God! I don't even know why I bother to answer you. You don't control me."

"That's where you're wrong." A smile stretched across his face and she was certain it had nothing whatsoever to do with pleasure.

"What do you mean, wrong?" A sick feeling of forewarning settled in her stomach, a lump ascending in her throat.

He swivelled round in the chair and rose to his feet, dominating her easily as he came around to the front of the desk. His proximity forced her to tip her head up to meet his black gaze. "I had an interesting time after I dropped you home on Saturday. A very interesting time indeed. You never told me that Evan was in the market to sell his shares in Davies Freight. Any particular reason you chose to not to let that snippet of information out during our…discussions?"

"I don't know what you're talking about."

"Of course you don't. Did he, or did he not, approach you on Friday to buy Brody's share of the business?"

"He did, but he never said anything about selling *his* share."

Mason rose one sceptical eyebrow, bringing Helena's blood to boiling point.

"What? What lies has he spun you?" Helena heard her voice rise in pitch, sounding frantic even to her own ears. "He's only after whatever he can get and if he thinks you believe him then he probably got exactly what he wanted."

"Oh, yeah. I think he got what he wanted." Mason drawled the figure he'd paid out to Evan. Helena's breath caught in her throat.

"You bought him out?"

"It was worth every cent. I've spent the past twelve hours assessing the position here and, Helena, it's not looking pretty."

"Of course it's not. I told you on Friday he was ruining the company. I asked you for your help."

"It's not that simple. I'm requesting a full audit."

Helena's shoulders relaxed in relief. Thank goodness she'd finally have some proof of Evan's scurrilous dealings. Once they found out what, exactly, he'd been doing, they could put into action a recovery plan. The sooner she could get onto that, the better. "I'll get you our accounting firm's number."

"That won't be necessary. I'll be calling in my own team of experts."

"But we've dealt with Flannigans for years. Patrick went to school with Ed Flannigan, for goodness sake."

"Which is exactly why we need a fresh eye on the books." Mason leaned a hip against the side of the desk and crossed his arms. "There's one other thing. Until the audit is completed you're suspended from your duties."

"Suspended? Why?"

"I don't want any question about your involvement, influence or otherwise, with this audit."

"So can I continue to work from home?"

Mason's brow furrowed and his eyes trapped her piercing intelligence. "Do you usually work from home?"

"Sometimes, yes. Patrick often did and I've found it necessary sometimes since he passed away. The computer at home is linked to the mainframe here. It just makes things easier, especially if something unexpected crops up after hours."

"I'll bet it does." Mason's comment was spoken so softly Helena wasn't even certain he'd said anything, but his next words rang loud and clear. "No. You won't be working from home anymore."

"That's ridiculous. Who's going to do my work? With Evan gone as well there won't be anyone here in authority."

"Except me."

"You? You have your own business to run. When will you have time?"

"You forget. This is my business now, at least half of it, anyway. I have perfectly capable managers at BKT who can reach me if they need to."

Helena kept her hands firmly at her sides—difficult to do when all she wanted was to bunch her fists and let loose some of the frustration bubbling up inside of her. "And will I still be on full pay during this suspension?"

Mason let out a laugh that had nothing to do with humour. "Money. It's always about the money with you, isn't it? Surely you have enough to manage on, or have you burned through all of Patrick's funds already?"

"Of course not! Patrick's estate is frozen, awaiting the grant of probate from the High Court. In the meantime I rely on my salary to meet day-to-day expenses. Brody's boarding fees are due this month, too."

"Well, they may not be your worry for much longer." Mason paused before continuing. "If the money's that important to you, then yes, you will still be on full pay."

"Thank you." He'd never have any idea how much it galled her to be discussing money like this right now. All through her childhood, they'd scrimped and scraped.

She'd sworn she'd never be a victim of straitened financial circumstance again.

Mason leaned across the desk and flipped the switch that put him through to reception. "Mandy? Would you send up the security detail I brought with me this morning?"

"Security?" Helena could only manage an incredulous whisper. "Is that really necessary?"

Mason ignored her question, his expression stony.

"The guards will take you to your office where you can get your bag. When you're done, I'll escort you home."

"Why are you doing this? It isn't what I asked of you at all." What lies had Evan poisoned him with? Now that her stepson had what money he wanted by selling out his shareholding to Mason, did he have to try to destroy her, too? The answer was painfully simple. Of course he did. It's what Evan did best. But even *he* probably couldn't have imagined that Mason would treat her this way. Like a criminal.

"You need to learn, Helena. I do things on my terms, no one else's."

A knock sounded at the door and two burly uniformed guards came in at Mason's request. Helena caught the Black Knight Transport logo on their sleeves, leaving her in no doubt that Mason meant every word he'd said. Already he was infiltrating Davies Freight with his staff. How long before her son's inheritance disappeared into the ether?

"You can't do this, it's…it's underhanded. You're raiding Brody's inheritance—robbing him. Stealing your own son's birthright!"

"Birthright? Isn't that exactly what's under examination? Right now, Helena, I'd advise you to be careful about who you hurl your insults at. Until Brody's parentage is confirmed keep your opinions to yourself, or you will find out exactly how underhanded I can be."

Helena stiffened at his threat but it wasn't enough to dampen the blaze of red-hot fury that flashed across her eyes. The old Helena would not have thought twice about lashing out to score her nails across that stony visage. The new Helena had to satisfy herself with imagining it. As if he could read her mind, Mason stepped forward, a tiny smile curling up one corner of his mouth.

"I wouldn't do it if I were you."

Helena shook with suppressed anger and clenched her hands into tight fists at her sides. She thrust her chin up and demanded, "Do what?"

"Whatever it was that made your eyes flash green fire just then. You know, Helena, if we're going to sort this out, you'll have to learn to control your temper better. Your expression is a dead giveaway to exactly what you're feeling. Don't ever take up poker." He nodded over to the guards. "Please escort Mrs. Davies to her office and see that she only removes what she arrived with this morning. Everything else is the property of Davies Freight."

"You're no different than him, no different at all," Helena spat before turning for the door.

"Than whom?"

"Evan. He always wanted what was Brody's, now you're doing exactly the same thing. I should never have asked for your help. Never!"

"Perhaps you should have come to that conclusion earlier, or maybe you should have approached one of your other lovers for help instead of me."

Other lovers? Nausea rose in her throat and she swallowed against the lump that lodged there. She dragged in one deep breath, then another.

"I beg your pardon. I don't think I understand you." She was relieved to hear her voice sounded measured and level, especially when she felt anything but. Was he accusing her of infidelity during her marriage to Patrick?

"Come on, Helena. What happened? Did they all say no? Was I your last resort?"

Helena stiffened her spine. She wouldn't dignify his accusations with an answer. Last resort? He'd been her only resort and that fact alone was enough to now make her truly fear, not only for her son's future, but also for her own.

Six

Lost for words, Helena spun on her heel and stalked to her office, followed closely by the guards. The gall of the man to even suggest that she'd take anything that wasn't hers, let alone suspend her from her job. A pain in the region of her heart made her reach for the portrait photo. This would never have happened if Patrick had listened to her and slowed down a bit more. If, for once, he'd done as the doctor had urged. Helpless tears filled her eyes but she willed them back and pressed her lips together to hide their telling tremble.

"I'm sorry, Ma'am, you can't take that."

"What?" Helena paused as the guard removed the framed photo from her hands and set it back down on the desk. "You must be kidding me."

"Orders from Mr. Knight. Nothing but what you came in with this morning."

"That's just ridiculous. Let me sort this out right this minute." She moved past the desk and made for her door, only to have her passage blocked by the unyielding form of one of the guards. "Move out of my way—now."

"If you're ready to leave, we'll escort you to the lobby."

"I am not ready to leave. I demand to speak to Mr. Knight. Get out of my way."

The door behind the guard opened and Mason's imposing figure filled the frame.

"Sorry, sir. But she wants to take the picture." The older of the two guards gestured at the portrait on her desk.

"Causing trouble, Helena? Why am I not surprised? Thank you, gentlemen, I'll see her out from here."

Helena stood in absolute silence as the two men left the room, her seething gaze locked on Mason's impassive face and her mind tumbling the words that clamoured for pole position out of her mouth. Without breaking eye contact she reached across the desk to where the guard had replaced the frame, and picked the photo up. She clutched the picture to her chest with one hand while grabbing at the strap of her shoulder bag and hooking up her suit jacket with the other.

"*Now* I'm ready to go."

Mason put out his hand. "Give it to me, Helena."

Oh, this was crazy. There was no way on this earth she was leaving here without the portrait. She pressed it more firmly against her breasts.

With an exasperated sigh, Mason's hand reached forward, his fingers brushing against hers as they curled around the frame. The proximity of his fingers to her skin, masked only by the silky blouse she wore, didn't go unnoticed either. Her breasts swelled in the lacy cups that held them, her nipples tightening almost immediately into hardened nubs. Her mouth dried as a visual image of his dark head bent over her breast burned across her retina. The moment's inattention was her undoing as he gave the frame a tiny tug, causing her to lose hold of it. She gave a small exclamation of dismay as the picture dropped from their collective grips and struck the corner of the desk with a sharp *crack* before hitting the carpeted floor.

"Oh, look what you've done." Helena bent swiftly to retrieve the picture before it could be cut by the shards of glass.

"Stop. Don't touch it." Mason grasped her hand just before she could lift the photo from the debris.

"It's all right, Mason. I think I can lift the photo up without cutting myself."

"That's not what I mean." He bent down and flicked over the backing of the frame, exposing a folded sheet of paper which had been tucked behind the photo.

Carefully he unfolded the sheet, the set of his mouth growing grim as he read the rows of numbers on the sheet.

"Let me see that." Helena reached for the paper.

"I don't think so. Was this what you were trying to smuggle out of here, Helena? Is this where all the money's been going?"

"What on earth are you talking about? What money?"

"Don't play the innocent with me. If there's one thing I'm sure you know all about, it's money."

A sick feeling settled deep in the pit of her stomach. "You're talking in riddles. I just want our photo. It's the last one I have of Patrick with Brody and me."

"I'll have it reframed for you and delivered to the house. Now come on. I want you out of here."

"Surely you're not suggesting I deliberately hid

something in that frame?" A mirthless laugh escaped her tightened throat. The sound flitted across the room before falling flat when she realised by his gaze that that was exactly what he was suggesting. "You're wrong. You have it all wrong."

"We'll see about that."

"Then you'll see you're wrong. About this, about me. About everything. I was faithful to Patrick. Always. Mind, heart and body. You can think what you like but I know the truth."

"I don't think you even know what the truth is anymore, Helena. In fact, I don't think you ever did."

"How dare you!"

"Oh, I dare." He flicked the sheet of paper with his fingers. "And I will get to the bottom of this. I hope you're prepared for what comes out because if I find so much as a hint that you've been stealing from Patrick all these years, you will be sorry you ever met him, or me."

"Sorry? I'm already sorry I met you."

"Good, then we both know exactly where we stand."

As they drove in frozen silence toward the waterfront suburb where Patrick had built Helena their home, Mason itched to get to the root of what those numbers were hiding, and if they matched up with his suspicions about Helena. Patrick had been a generous man. More than generous. Mason could only be grateful that his mentor had never suspected his beautiful trophy wife of such duplicitous behaviour. The truth would have devastated him.

He took his eyes off the road long enough to flick a glance her way. Helena sat, locked in her thoughts, beside him. Her skin was pale, almost translucent, and dark shadows scored rings under her eyes. This morning had come as quite a shock to her, that much was obvious. Something she'd said earlier tickled at the back of his mind.

"You mentioned the paternity testing before. What did you find out?"

He felt her start as his words broke the frigid air between them.

"The testing lab is right here in Auckland. It's quite straightforward. You pay your money, you get your test."

"How much?"

Helena told him the figure she'd been given over the phone.

"So when are we going?" he pressed.

"I haven't booked it yet." Helena sounded surprised.

"Don't you want to know now, or is it that you're frightened I'm going to find you out for a liar?" His fingers tightened on the wheel as they turned into her gates and swung up the cobbled drive to the front of her house.

"I'm not afraid of anything, Mason Knight, particularly not the truth. Maybe that's something you should try sometime before jumping to asinine conclusions."

"I call it as I see it until I know differently. How soon can we get the results?"

"They said their general time frame is three weeks but apparently in most cases the results are available within a few days."

Mason drummed his fingers on the steering wheel. A few days. In only a few days he could find out whether he had a son. A son he knew only from a few boastful photographs shared by Patrick after a business meeting. A son he'd deserved to know from birth. The hollowness that had taken residence deep inside his chest since he'd learned he might be Brody's father ached anew. All those wasted years. If it was true, it wasn't only Helena who'd cheated him out of fatherhood, it had been his mentor, too. The betrayal didn't bear considering. Patrick had known him even better, perhaps, than his own father—he alone would have known what this news would do to him, the toll it would take. He shut the door firmly on that part of his mind and focussed on the present.

"What's involved?"

"All we need is recent photo identification of the parties involved and we can either have the samples taken at the laboratory itself or at any local diagnostic collection room."

"That simple, huh?"

Helena sighed. "Yeah. I thought it would be more complex. But all they need is the consent forms completed and either a blood sample or a swab of your mouth."

"Book it."

"I can't just do it like that."

His ire rose at her protest. "Why the hell not?" He ground the words past his teeth. She'd taken it this far. The only reason she wouldn't go all the way now was if she was having second thoughts. As far as he was concerned it was way too late for them now.

"I have Brody to consider."

"Yeah, so?"

"Well, I don't want to upset him. He doesn't need to know yet that Patrick wasn't his father. He's just coming to terms with his grief. I can't do that to him. I need to tread carefully here."

"Helena, if you don't organise this within the next few days, I can promise you that I will take whatever steps are necessary to have Brody tested."

"You can't!"

"Don't push me."

He watched as she lifted a hand to her hair, and absently twirled a hank until it wound like a corkscrew. A shudder ran through him as he remembered the texture of that hair—like warm, russet coloured silk—through his fingers, across his body. A sharp jolt of desire burned a trail below his belt. He hated that she could incite such a reaction in him.

Mason let go the breath he'd drawn in a frustrated rush of air. "I'm not negotiable on this, Helena. You came to me for help. I want proof."

"I might be able to get him tested at school, but I'm not telling him why. Not yet."

"Frankly, at this stage I don't care what you tell him. Just get it done."

"Fine. Is that everything then, *master?*"

The sarcasm in her voice was just enough to tip him over the edge. Ever since he'd dropped her home on Saturday she'd plagued his mind and body. The sooner he got this wretched physical yearning for her out of his system, the better. Denying himself the satisfaction of release on Friday night had been a bad move. It only served to make him want her more.

"Everything? Not by a long shot."

Mason hooked one arm around her shoulders and pulled her to him, his other hand reaching behind her head, grabbing the fullness of her hair and tilting her face to meet his onslaught. From the split-second it took to identify the fear in her emerald gaze to the moment his lips touched hers, he was driven by anger—by the need to dominate and force her to submit to him. But as her soft lips parted in surprise beneath his and his mouth filled with the heady intoxicating taste of her, the fury left his body, leaving it replaced instead by something far more dangerous. Something that threatened his equilibrium in a way nothing and no one else ever had.

She tasted of some sweet feminine blend he couldn't get enough of—a taste that was intrinsically her own. His tongue swept past her lips to stroke against hers, to entice her to take him deeper. She moaned from deep down in her throat and the sound drove him crazy. She was his for the taking. He should be disgusted that it was so easy—that she was so easy for him—but all he wanted was more. More of her mouth, more of her body, more of her heat.

He lifted his head and watched as she opened her eyes—the green depths hazy with desire, her pupils dilated to enormous black pools.

"Let's take this inside," he growled.

The change in her expression was as immediate and as chilling as a hail storm.

"Let's not."

Before he could stop her, she'd gathered her things and was out of the car.

Mason climbed from the vehicle and leaned over the roof, watching as she all but ran for the sanctuary of her front door. "You can run from me, Helena, but it's not over between us until I say so," he called after her retreating form.

She hesitated for a moment in the portico, her key already slotting into the front door. For a second he thought she'd turn and say something, anything, but with a flick of her wrist the door was open and she stepped inside. The resounding bang as it closed behind her retreating form echoed across the drive.

Helena watched from behind the sheer curtains in the front room as, for a full thirty seconds, Mason didn't move. Then, to her relief, he got back into the car and roared away—gravel spitting out from under his tyres.

One touch, that's all it took, and she'd melted for him again. Her body still clamoured for his. She had to shore her reserves against him somehow. She turned from the window and raced up the stairs to her bedroom and discarded her clothing in an untidy heap. As cold as the swimming pool would be, anything would be preferable to the flaming heat that seared her veins. She grabbed a black one-piece swimsuit from the drawer and pulled it on over her body, groaning slightly as the fabric caressed her breasts. Had she done as Mason had suggested, it would be his hands, his mouth, his tongue, caressing her now. And maybe, just maybe, the ever tightening knot of need that had plagued her since Friday night would begin to be assuaged.

But she'd said no, and she'd run, because she knew deep down inside that if he'd touched her once more she'd have conceded to his power over her, and done so willingly.

Her inner muscles clenched tight against the tingle of desire deep inside. Even now she wanted him, even when he so clearly despised her and had believed whatever web of lies Evan had spun. Without pausing for another thought Helena barrelled down the stairs and through the house to the indoor pool. She hadn't bothered to keep it heated since Patrick's death and the sluicing coolness would be just what her body needed right now. About twenty laps should do it, she thought haphazardly, or maybe a hundred. Whatever it took, she wasn't getting out of that pool until she felt as weak as jelly and as incapable of submitting to Mason Knight as possible.

* * *

Rain-laden skies threatened overhead, turning the late afternoon into premature night. She hoped the weather would hold off. They had the last appointment at the clinic and would miss it if the weather, and subsequently the Auckland city traffic, turned foul. Helena stood nervously in the brightly-lit portico at her front door waiting for the roar of Mason's Porsche to come up her drive. She hadn't spoken to him since a week ago on Monday when he'd driven her home. A computer forensics company had turned up at her door, just as she'd finished her gruelling marathon in the pool, to take the computer from the library and since then she'd had no contact with work at all.

The first day home had stretched out interminably and finally boredom had driven her to start going through Patrick's personal items—packing up his clothes and things that neither Brody nor Evan would want into boxes for local charities, and setting aside other items Patrick had listed in his will as bequests for Evan and some of his old friends. It had been a job she'd been putting off—the finality of it almost too much to bear. The boxes now stood, stacked like sentinels, just inside her front entrance. A physical reminder of Patrick's absence from her life.

She didn't want to think about that right now. Today would be trial enough without dealing anew with her grief. When she'd booked the appointment at the laboratory, in defiance and knowing Mason could be contacted at Davies Freight, she had deliberately left a message with his secretary at Black Knight Transport about where they had to be and when.

Caller ID had saved her from having to speak with

him when he'd called back to confirm he'd be picking her up to take her for their tests. The tone of his voice on the answering machine left her in no doubt that he suspected she was standing there, listening, and refusing to pick up the phone to speak with him personally. She'd almost hoped she could get away with taking a taxi and meeting him there, but acceded that it would only be prolonging the inevitable. She had to face him some time, somewhere.

In the distance she heard the downshift of gears as a car approached from the road and a sweep of headlights lit the foliage that lined the long driveway—it may as well be now.

As he swung the gleaming low-slung vehicle around her turning bay, she stepped out toward the car. Nerves bundled into ever-tightening knots as she reached out to open the door and settled herself inside. With nothing but a curt nod from Mason, they were on their way. Fortunately, the threatening rain held off, but despite the fact that the laboratory was a mere twenty minutes from her home, every kilometre passed in painful thickening silence. Finally, she could stand it no longer.

"So? Have you found out everything you need to prove I'm a liar yet?" she challenged.

"Not yet."

"That's because there's nothing there."

"We'll see." Mason pulled the car up in the parking lot outside the laboratory. "What have you arranged for Brody?"

"I told Brody our family doctor was concerned with how lethargic he's been lately." That in itself was no lie, although their doctor had also hastened to add that at Brody's stage of adolescent development it wasn't unusual, especially combined with his grief over losing the only father he'd ever known. The doctor had advised Helena to ask the school nurse to keep an eye on him and they could take further action later if necessary.

"And?" Mason prompted.

"And I told him that the doctor wanted to be sure he hadn't contracted glandular fever and had requested blood work be done. I don't appreciate having to lie to my son."

"Why start worrying about that now? You've lied to him his entire life." The acrid bitterness in Mason's voice flayed her like a whip and she physically recoiled from him.

"I didn't know Patrick wasn't his father until his lawyer gave me his medical records. Why won't you believe me?"

"Because I really have no cause to believe you, Helena."

"Well, you'll have to believe me when we get the results of these tests."

"All they will prove is that either you're lying now or that you've cheated me out of my son's life for the past eleven years. Frankly, I don't find anything admirable in either of them. Do you?"

"I didn't know!"

Mason ignored her as he alighted from the car and came around to open her door. "Come on. At least this will get us one step closer to the truth."

Helena walked by his side, his hand at her elbow as they entered the building. Fleetingly she wondered how many couples the staff here saw arriving like this—couples filled with anxiety at the outcome of the test. In her heart, she knew the result couldn't be anything but proof that Mason was Brody's father. She hadn't been with anyone in almost a year prior to her marriage to Patrick—no one except Mason.

The memory of that night, of the raw passion that had driven her, drove a spike of pure longing from her core and through her entire body. It had been an instinctive reaction to the trauma she'd been through, she understood that now. She'd read every book on the topic in a vain attempt to identify what had driven her uncharacteristic behaviour that night. The fact that it could be pigeonholed by psychobabble was little comfort in the face of Mason's behaviour, however.

He barely spoke to her as they went through the process of confirming their identification and completing the forms and consents. The test itself was almost disappointingly simple. Helena felt that for something so momentous it should have been more complex, more time-consuming. More important, somehow. Once the samples were taken they were free to go. Free to wait for what would arguably be the three longest days of her life.

Now, as they walked out to the car in a silence that was anything but companionable, she felt the tension begin anew. As she buckled her car seat belt, she sighed.

"Too late for second thoughts," Mason stated, turning to face her with a flare of challenge in his eyes.

"I'm not having second thoughts."

The expression on Mason's face told her clearly he thought she was lying, and since that was basically what he thought about everything that came out of her mouth, she had retrained herself not to care—much.

"I'm not scared of the truth," she insisted. *At least not in the way you think,* she added silently. When she'd initially approached Mason it had been with the sole intention of securing Brody's inheritance and seeing that Patrick's wishes were carried out. But, in the face of his animosity toward her, she'd been rattled by an even more disturbing consideration.

What if Mason wanted to take fatherhood a step further? What if he wanted to take Brody away from her?

While a part of her mind argued that surely no family court in New Zealand would allow such a thing, she knew it wouldn't take too much digging to expose the piece of her past that would sit like a big black mark against her. Digging, ha! If Evan knew, the whole world could know in only a matter of moments. She swallowed against the obstruction lodged between her throat and her chest like a malignant knot of fear. She couldn't afford to even think about that happening.

Patrick had had his reasons, whatever they were, for not telling Mason about his son any earlier. He would never have shared that information if he'd dreamed it could see her lose the human being most dear to her. Since their marriage her relationship with her parents had become strained, and her contact with them had become less frequent. It was something that brought her plenty of sleepless nights, dogged with guilt, but they'd seemed happy enough in their own world. A world Patrick had paid for, not that they knew that. The older her parents had become, the more insular they'd grown and their relief that she was financially off their hands had been huge.

Besides, she knew Patrick couldn't have lied to her about his infertility. He had neither cause nor advantage to have done so. In his letter to her he'd told her how he'd figured it out after seeing the logs of the radio conversation Mason had had with the controllers at the depot that night. How he'd saved a young woman's life and returned to her safety. Given that Patrick knew she'd lost her car on the journey north, it hadn't taken him long to figure out what might have happened when she'd told him she was pregnant. In Helena's opinion, it said a lot for Patrick's strength as a man that he'd accepted Brody as his own.

Mason was Brody's father no matter how much he distrusted her. That distrust, however, still kept her from her duties at Davies Freight. Every day she'd worried and wondered how things were going, whether Mason was any closer to discovering the soak hole that was draining the company's financial stability.

"How are things at work?" Helena switched subjects.

"I already told you. Nothing conclusive yet."

"I don't mean the investigation. What about the staff, how are they handling the changes?" Patrick had taken a personal interest in all his staff, each one handpicked for their position. In their own way they were an extension of his family, and he respected everyone who worked for him accordingly.

"Pretty well. There's been a bit of confusion but they're all keen to save their jobs. I had a meeting this week with the core team to discuss options."

"Without me?"

"Obviously."

"I should have been there." She bit her lip, forcing back the words that begged to be spoken. When Patrick had died so suddenly, the staff had turned to her for guidance within the company. With both of them gone it would be like sailing a ship without a skipper. Or, at the very least, with a man at the helm they probably had genuine reason to fear. If it became Mason's intention to merge the two companies at least half of her staff's positions would go. Worse, if he found the company was unsustainable, everyone would lose their job. "Are you talking redundancies yet?"

"Hopefully not at all. Once the audit is complete we'll know better where we stand. Suffice to say, whatever put Davies Freight in the position it's in appears to have stagnated." He threw her a telling glance.

"I suppose you think that's because I'm not there."

"Looks that way."

"Evan's not there either," Helena hastened to point out, trying to ignore the chill that swept her skin. She'd battled over the past few weeks to find the source of the problem, but it appeared too deeply entrenched in the system. Evan's flashy lifestyle had pointed the finger firmly in his direction and she was certain he was the culprit. That, combined with his sudden desire to sell after Patrick died, supported her theory. Somehow he'd gotten in too deep and need a large cash influx fast. And now he had it, from Mason.

"Worried I'm catching up to your schemes, Helena?"

"No! When will you understand? It's not me that's under question here. It's Evan."

"Funny, that's what he implied about you before accepting my cheque."

"How can you still believe him over me?"

Mason turned into her driveway and pulled the car up to a halt at her front door.

He sighed and turned off the motor, then rested his fisted hands on the steering wheel. "I don't know what to believe anymore, Helena."

Finally. A chink in his armour. Helena would've rejoiced in his indecision if for one second she thought it would do her any good. Instead, that one small indication of frailty, of uncertainty, made her wonder if she shouldn't be even more worried than before. Always, Mason had been steadfast. Focussed. Determined. She reached out a hand and rested it on his. The warmth of his skin was instantly absorbed into hers and sent a spreading heat through her arm.

"Believe the facts. Believe the truth." She squeezed his tightly fisted fingers gently. "Please, believe me."

Seven

The air between them crackled with tension as her words hovered before fading away to nothing. She'd had absolutely no impact on him if his expression was anything to go by.

Mason listened to the earnest tone in her voice. Any other man would capitulate at this point, he was certain. Any other man but him. He'd been victim to the honeyed suggestions of another lying female before and the fallout had been devastating. It had set him apart from his family and put him on his solitary road to success. His elder brother, Declan, had branched out on his own—away from the umbrella of their father's company—but even he still had more in common with the old man than he realised. Of course Connor had stayed within the family fold once he'd attained his law degree. He'd been too young, and Declan too knowing, to fall for the attention teasingly scattered Mason's way by Melanie, his father's much younger mistress.

No, it was only him. The black sheep of the family. The loner. That was probably what had made him a prime target for Melanie's manipulation of a teenage boy's wild crush. For the devastation it had wrought on his relationship with his dad. No, he wouldn't believe Helena Davies. Not until he had quantifiable proof that she was as innocent as she claimed.

"Mason?" She broke into his thoughts.

"What?"

"Would you like to come in for coffee before you head back?"

"Sure." He clamped down his surprise at her sudden offer. She'd avoided all contact with him this past week, now she was inviting him inside the house. In itself, that made him suspicious. So he'd play her game. As the saying went, "Keep Your Friends Close. Keep Your Enemies Closer."

Mason's shoulders stiffened as they entered through the ornately carved front door and into the tiled entranceway. He almost expected Patrick to come through from the formal sitting room area, booming his welcome. God, he missed him.

"It's almost like he's still here, isn't it?" Helena spoke softly, a thread of tears in her voice. "I feel the same way every time I come through that door."

"Yeah. He's kind of hard to forget."

They walked into the kitchen in silence.

"How did you meet Patrick?" Helena asked.

"He never told you?"

"At the wedding, when I saw you standing there…well, suffice to say I never asked." Helena bent her head as she filled the jug at the kitchen sink, her hair obscuring her expression.

Mason would have liked to have seen her face right at this minute. He'd lay odds it was a darn sight more expressive than it had been that afternoon when she'd come floating down the aisle of the cathedral, an ethereal vision of beauty. A beauty that belied the bedraggled creature he'd pulled from certain death only hours before. The calm serenity on her face at complete odds with the driving passion of her body as she'd ridden him in the darkest hours of the night.

The memory of that passion stirred him anew, making his skin heat with need and his body tighten with a coiling hunger that whorled deep inside.

"Milk?"

"What? Oh, yeah. Just a bit, thanks. We met when I came out of the army. I responded to a call for owner drivers at the time. I was young, full of balls and bursting to make my own mark on the world." He laughed, a short harsh sound that had nothing to do with humour. "I didn't even have my own truck. I rolled up to the depot with nothing but a dream and a plan. Anyone else would have sent me on my way, or laughed so hard their gut would've burst, but not Patrick. No, he listened. Then he outlined a plan where I could do exactly what I wanted to do. What I needed to do."

To his horror, his voice broke on the last words. For a moment he was that defensive young man once more, searching for a means by which he could purge his anger and disappointment. He cleared his throat before continuing.

"Anyway, he made things happen for me."

"Mason, I'm so sorry."

"Sorry?"

"He meant so much to you and I took him from you, didn't I? If I hadn't slept with you that night, you would have seen more of him, spent more time with him. Heaven knows, maybe he'd even have listened to you instead of ignoring me when I asked him to cut back on his workload—to start to hand over the reins."

"And who would he have handed them over to, Helena? Evan? You? It's no wonder he worked himself to death." Mason flung an arm out, gesturing toward her home and possessions. "He worked for you, for this. For what you wanted."

"No. No, it wasn't like that." Tears glistened in her eyes.

"Wasn't it? Until he married you he was happy with less."

"Mason, you know what he was like. Don't let your bitterness toward me cloud your memory of Patrick. He was the most generous of men. Look at yourself. Look at what he did for you. Can you honestly say you'd be where you are now if he hadn't believed in you and what you believed you could achieve? Okay, so maybe you'd have gotten there eventually, but I'd lay odds that it wouldn't have been that fast." She rubbed at her eyes with a haphazard swipe. Even as she denuded her face of the evidence of her emotion he heard the change of tone in her voice—from soft and cajoling to hard and concise. "Be angry at me, for sure, but don't take what he gave you away. You both deserve more than that."

Her words chipped at him like a hammer and chisel, eventually fracturing the shell he worked so hard to build over his wounded heart. The pain of loss swamped him anew, mingled with the anger he'd been harbouring, not only against Patrick for marrying Helena, but also against his father for believing Melanie over him when he'd finally confronted them both. The ensuing argument had seen him become a pariah in his own home, while Melanie had sat like the cat who'd gotten the cream. Smug that her sexual prowess had allowed her to manipulate not only an older man, but his son as well.

That his relationship with Patrick had ended up destroyed as history repeated itself had come as an unbelievable blow. But this time, the responsibility had been his and his alone. He hadn't been the love-struck teenager of his youth. He'd been a young man on the fast road to success. He could've spoken up to stop Patrick from marrying Helena. He'd chosen not to, and then he'd chosen to allow himself to be closed away. His contact with his mentor diminishing each year until they barely saw or spoke to one another anymore in the months leading up to Patrick's death.

"You're right." His voice sounded foreign, strained, even to his own ears.

"Right?"

"Yeah. You took him from me." He watched as she flinched, her eyes filled with shock at his bluntness. "But worse than that, I let you."

"I never wanted to come between you. Until I married Patrick I had no idea who you were, or how close you were to him." He watched as she automatically went through the process of making their coffee, not even aware of what she was doing until a drop of hot water backwashed from the mug she was pouring into and splashed painfully against her hand. She jumped, dropping the mug onto the counter top. As the liquid began to spill across the dark granite surface she reached for a cloth.

"You need to get cold water on that."

"I'll be fine."

Mason rounded the kitchen bench and grabbed her hand, pulling her gently toward the sink and running the cold tap water over her reddening skin. She tried to pull her fingers from his grasp but he held her firmly as the cooling water did its work to pull the heat from the burn.

Helena closed her eyes, compliant at his touch. One minute they were arguing and the next she was the recipient of his care. The paradoxical situation was enough to make her want to weep. But there'd been enough tears. For Patrick, for Brody—and yes, even for Mason. No more. She was wrung out.

"How does that feel now?" His head was so close to hers his breath brushed against her hair, the sensation sending a trickle of awareness like a warning signal down her neck with a shiver.

"Okay. It's fine. You can let go of me now."

Their proximity was at once intimate, yet impersonal. His body covered hers from behind, his hips cradling her buttocks. Helena could barely breathe. Every nerve in her body almost painfully attuned to the heat radiating off his body, to the hard-muscled plane of his stomach pressed against her back.

"I—I think that's enough now," she murmured. Surely now he'd back off. Stop this mental and physical torment. He was so much bigger than her, so much stronger, although she didn't feel intimidated as much by his size as she was by her own craving for him. A craving that went soul deep. She prayed he'd back away.

Mason flicked off the tap with his free hand and, still

holding her injured one gently in his, reached across for a towel. Helena held her breath, waiting for the sting as he carefully dried the moisture off her hand. But the sting never came.

Instead, she only felt the soft pressure of Mason's lips. Her fingers curled involuntarily around his, the words she desperately needed to utter—to beg him to stop—stuttered to a halt in her throat. All pain fled as his tongue snaked out and trailed a path along the back of her hand. Her knees turned to water as he turned her wrist and laved his tongue across her pulse point before covering the wetness with his lips.

"Mason?" His name sighed from her, like a plea.

"Yes?"

"Don't, please don't. We're not ready for this. Not now. Not yet."

"Ready, Helena?" He tilted her chin with one finger so she looked directly up into his eyes, eyes that glowed with a molten heat that seared right through to her core. "When it comes to you, I'm so ready it hurts."

Her heart fluttered in her chest. This was too much, especially when she was still raw from the painful aftermath of the night when they'd begun to make love, only to have it end with such wrenching desolation. She wasn't ready. Not for this.

"I can't. *We* can't."

"Scared?" He bent his head and pressed a kiss against the corner of her mouth before fleetingly darting his tongue across her lower lip.

Terrified was the word that immediately sprang to mind. But for the life of her she couldn't pull away.

He was like a drug. Once sampled, instantly addicted. Oh sure, she thought she'd conquered this addiction, but twelve years of marriage to a man she'd loved and revered had merely dulled the hunger.

A warning flashed in the back of her mind. Would Mason just use her weakness against her and fling her clawing desire for him back into her face? She had to take the risk, had to give in to the overpowering craving to be with him every way she could.

Mason kissed her again, this time coaxing her lips apart with a pressure that hinted at the power behind his restraint.

"Don't worry, I'll hold you."

She was in his arms and they were ascending the stairs before she realised she'd even so much as whispered the word *yes*. As he neared her bedroom door she stiffened in his arms.

"No, not in there. Please. One of the guest rooms."

At her request, Mason strode the short distance down the carpeted hallway, the sound of his footsteps swallowed by the thick pile of the carpet. At the door to the furthermost guest room he slowly lowered her, allowing her to drag against his body as her feet found the floor, making sure she was left with no doubt about his desire for her. His hardness was an insistent pressure against her belly. Knowing she had such an effect on him both empowered and awed her.

This strong, vital man wanted her. He'd wanted her before, that first time, although she had to admit that she had taken advantage of him. Taken his chance to make a choice away from him, almost as she'd taken Patrick away from him. Hearing Mason talk back there in the kitchen finally brought it home to her what a devastating effect she'd had on him. Worse, she'd unwittingly taken from him his chance to be a father to their son.

She owed him—everything—and she had to make it up to him, as much as she could. That making up started now.

Instinctively, Helena reached for the doorknob behind her, turned it, and pushed open the door. She took each of Mason's hands in her own and, walking slowly backward, she drew him into the room. Mason kicked the door shut behind them. Helena reached for the light switch.

"Don't."

"But I want to see you," she protested softly.

"Leave it off. I want…I want it to be like the first time."

"Our first time?"

"Shh." He grazed her lips with one finger. "No more talking."

Helena's eyes hadn't even adjusted to the dark when his mouth closed on hers, his hand sliding up her back to the nape of her neck and holding her against him as if his life depended on her. She opened her mouth to his assault, and in that moment, opened her heart to him as she'd never allowed herself to ever before. The emotion that turbulently cascaded within her was nothing like the strong secure love she'd shared with Patrick. Love? Was this crazy roller coaster of feeling she went through every time she thought about Mason, love?

If it was, she wanted more. More than this moment of lovemaking, this slaking of their lust for one another that even after twelve years burned as hot and vivid as it had that one fateful night. The truth tore through her, sweeping away reason, opening the floodgates of her desire once again.

She lifted her hands to his face, and drove her fingers through his hair, the blunt cut strands grazing against her palms. Every thought, every sensation was heightened. Every particle of her focussed solely on Mason Knight.

Impatient hands pushed at her clothing with scant regard for fasteners or zips. On the periphery of her passion she heard and felt the buttons pop from her knitted top but she didn't care. She had an agenda of her own—to feel his skin against hers again, as quickly as possible. In moments they were both naked, their bodies aligned against one another. The hard, hot skin of his erection pulsed against her bare belly and a new wave of need radiated through her body from her centre to her very fingertips.

Mason's hands cupped her buttocks, lifting her hard against him, positioning her so the throbbing tip of him nudged against the slick hot entrance to her body.

A groan tore from his throat, feral in its ferocity. "Protection."

One word that could halt them in their tracks. One word that should have hammered home its message to her that night in his truck, in the warmth of his comforting embrace. One word she knew she could deliver on this time.

"It's okay, I'm on the pill."

For a moment Mason allowed a single stray thought into his head. Patrick had let on one night over drinks that the physical side of his marriage had all but ended. Was it consideration for her husband's erratic libido, in the belief that he was still fertile, that had her on the pill, or was it so she could keep her lovers without a care for any consequences? He didn't want to think of that now, now when his body wound ever tighter, demanding release. Demanding surcease from the ever-present tension he knew would only ease if he satisfied his hunger for her. For now it didn't matter if she had other lovers, so long as he had her.

Then, his senses went on full alert. The air in front of him moved with a shimmering heat. A question rose in his throat, only to stall, unsaid, as small warm hands cupped his balls, stroking and kneading with a firm, gentle rhythm. Anticipation almost made him jump out of his skin as the hot, wet stroke of her tongue started at the base of his arousal, the merest touch enough to make his body jerk and thrust forward.

He'd been a fool to keep the lights off. Right now he'd give anything to watch her, to see her expression as she stroked her tongue in tiny flicks from base to just below the tip of his penis. Then her lips closed over the head. She stilled and for a moment he simply relished the heat of her mouth, the texture of her tongue as she swirled it about his shaft. He was about to explode. He had to hold back—he hadn't waited for her for twelve years merely to lose it in twelve seconds.

With a raw growl he pushed his hands in her hair— fighting the urge to plunge against her—instead withdrawing from her heat and reaching for her, to pull her upright.

"I want to be inside you, to feel you."

"Like the last time?"

Her voice was unsure and he briefly felt a twinge of unease, a hint of regret for how he'd treated her the last time they were so intimate.

"No. Like the first."

He swept her into his arms again and carefully made his way in the dark to the bed. Laying her down on the covers he knelt down on the bed next to her. Helena's voice whispered through the darkness.

"If it's going to be like the first time, then you have to pretend to be asleep."

"Pretend? I wasn't pretending."

"So pretend now." Her breath stroked across his cheek.

"Is that an order?"

"If it needs to be."

His skin raised with goose bumps as her breath travelled down his chest, over his nipples, past his navel. Small deft fingers sheathed him, then, mercifully, the mattress shifted as she positioned herself over his body. Without hesitation she slid down the full length of him until they were joined, almost seamlessly. Sensation poured through him, pushing at the edges of his control. He had to last the distance.

A deep sense of rightness rocked through Helena as she settled her body over Mason's, as she drew him deep inside to her inner core. He completed her physically. Their joining felt so right. Gently she undulated against him, feeling the restraint within him that held him still as she increased the depth of her movements. Swells of pleasure grew in intensity, rising and falling through her body until she no longer felt in control. Only felt the instinctive need to ride the current of longing that craved release.

Mason's hands gripped her hips, his fingers digging into her skin, holding her firmly, not allowing her to withdraw from the journey they took together. Suddenly, she could bear it no longer. All control fled as sensation built to a peak and then poured, molten through her veins. Her body slicked with perspiration as she rocked harder, every movement silently imploring for release.

As slowly as the tension had risen, pleasure began to radiate through her body, her climax growing in strength, building like a giant wall of colour, heat and light until it crashed with terminal velocity through every nerve in her body. Mason thrust upward then shuddered against her as she collapsed against him, her body vibrating with the eruption of release.

Mason wrapped his arms around her, holding her so close she felt as though she were moulded to him. Against her ear, his heart thudded in rapid beats in his chest. His lungs drew in great gulps of air. Helena sighed in satisfaction, her eyelids drooping in sheer physical exhaustion. As she drifted off to sleep hope began to grow within that maybe, finally, she could start to make things right with him.

More than that, she *wanted* to make things right with him. It went beyond the sex. She wanted much more than that. She wanted the chance to make up to him all she'd inadvertently denied him—from his lost years with Brody, to the lost chance she'd had to love him as he deserved to be loved.

Eight

Mason woke to rumpled sheets and an empty bed. Despite the fact they'd slept little during the night, somehow he felt more rested—more satisfied—than he had in years. He got up and made his way into the guest bathroom, taking a quick hot shower before dragging on the clothes that lay strewn about the room.

Downstairs, he found Helena in the family room— her fingers wrapped tight about a large coffee mug and a stack of books in front of her on the coffee table. A flush of colour painted her cheeks as he came in, brightening the green glitter of her eyes. His gut clenched. She was an incredibly beautiful woman. Her looks deceptively fragile. Although she'd lost weight since Patrick's death, and looked as though it would take little more than a strong sou'-westerly to knock her off her feet, he recognised that her backbone was made of pure steel.

She was strong, she was tough, she was smart. If they'd met under the right circumstances who knew where they'd be now?

"Good morning." He leaned down and kissed her, hard. Desire flamed instantly. Even after their lovemaking last night he still hadn't slaked his hunger for her. He wanted her now even more.

"Let me get you some coffee." She started to get up but he gently pushed her back down in her seat.

"No problem. I can help myself. You look like you've been busy." He gestured toward the stack of books on the coffee table in front of her.

"I gathered some albums I thought you might like to go through."

"Albums?"

"Of Brody. You didn't come over much after Patrick and I married. You missed so much."

A searing shaft of anger stabbed through him, quenching his desire as effectively as an extinguisher on a fire. Did she seriously think a few photographs would make up for the lost years if Brody proved to be his son? Mason swallowed back the retort he knew would flay her to shreds.

"Take a seat. The albums are in chronological order."

"Look, Helena, now's probably not a good time. Why don't we wait until we know for sure?"

Helena rose from her seat and tipped the remnants of her coffee in the sink. He saw a shiver go through her body. She kept her back to him as she spoke, her hands gripping the bench, her face staring out the kitchen window.

"Are you afraid of the truth, Mason? Is that why you won't look at the albums?" She turned abruptly and locked her temptress's green gaze with his. "He's more like you than you could imagine, you know. Now that I know the truth, I can see it in him. *He is your son.*"

As far as he could tell there was no guile, no deception in her clear-eyed stare. No, there was nothing there but challenge. Damn her. She knew he wouldn't ignore the gauntlet once thrown down. Even their lovemaking last night had been like that. Challenge, counter challenge. Driving one another to new heights of pleasure.

He was having a hard enough time adjusting to the fact that taking her body hadn't eased the driving hunger in his—was even beginning to wonder just how much it would take before he'd had enough of Helena Davies. And now she wanted to throw this into the equation.

Fine then. He'd pick up the challenge. He threw himself into the comfortable sofa in front of the coffee table. Late morning winter sun beamed watery rays across the table, illuminating the collection of albums there, each painstakingly labelled in Helena's copperplate-style handwriting with Brody's name and the dates. Mason slid the album nearest him off the stack and flipped open the pages. A photo of her—almost naked and proudly displaying her swollen bare belly—sucked every last vestige of breath from his lungs.

The picture was deeply intimate, yet sensual at the same time. The joy in her eyes and the possessive touch of her hand on the lush curve of her stomach were both offset by a forest green strip of satin that was swathed lovingly across the fullness of her breasts and around her body, trailing under the mound that protected the new life inside. The shimmer of light and dark on the fabric drew his eye across her figure in a way that celebrated the joining of two bodies to result in new life and motherhood.

Desire flowed with thick heat through his veins as his eyes devoured the flush of warmth on her creamy skin, the hidden promise of her beauty beneath the satin, of the ripe enticing shape of her. If Brody was his, she'd cheated him of this—of watching her grow full with his baby, his son. No matter what came now, he'd never have that time back.

He could finally identify his anger toward Helena for what it really was. She'd taken a vital piece of him with her the morning after he'd saved her life. She'd taken his hope, then she'd encased it in ice as cold and brilliant as the diamonds of the wedding band placed on her finger by another man. A man she should never have married.

Mason slowly worked through each album, turning the pages one by one, his vision blurring as the pictures of a newborn baby with indistinct features firmed and shaped as Brody matured, until Mason knew without a doubt that he was staring at his own image in a younger form. He blinked away the moisture from his eyes, refusing to give in to such weakness in her presence, determined instead to feed on the energy that welled in frustrated fury from deep inside him.

He closed the final page on the album and looked up. Words failed him. Across the table from him, Helena sat, silver tear tracks shining on her cheeks.

"I wish I'd known then," she said, brokenly. "You deserve more than this. More than a photographic summary of Brody's life."

"That still remains to be seen." Even though he knew the words for a lie, he had to give them voice. In his heart, to the depths of his soul, he understood this child was his, and understood why he'd fought so hard to deny it. Feeling cheated didn't even begin to describe how raw he felt inside right now.

"Why are you so stubborn? Why can't you just accept it?"

"Accept it? Accept that the man I admired more than my own father betrayed me? Accept that you slept with me, allowed me to impregnate you, and then married someone else and let him raise my son as his own?" Mason pushed back his chair, the legs skidding across the terracotta-tiled floor with the force with which he stood. "You ask too much."

He covered the distance between the kitchen and the front door in a haze of anger, oblivious to the soft pad of Helena's bare feet on the floor as she followed him.

"Mason, wait!"

He ignored her and pulled open the front door with a wrench that did little to assuage the tension that controlled him. He had to get out of here. Away from the memories of Patrick Davies, away from Helena and as far away as possible from the truth he couldn't deny.

It no longer mattered how long the paternity test results took. He would put matters in motion today to ensure that he attained sole custody of the boy. By the time he was through with Helena she would wish she'd never been born.

Several days later, Mason stood in his office at Black Knight Transport and turned an envelope over and over in his hands. The discreet logo of the diagnostic laboratory taunted him. Now that the moment of truth had come, for some crazy reason he was reluctant to know the outcome of the paternity test. Not that it mattered anymore, anyway. In his heart he knew he was Brody's father. The albums he'd leafed through last week had convinced him beyond a shadow of a doubt and had made the family gathering he'd endured at his father's place this past weekend, together with his brothers and their expanding families, all the more stilted and painful.

At Connor's suggestion, he'd spoken with one of Auckland's foremost solicitors in family law. He had an outside chance, at best, of removing Brody from Helena's care, but as far as he was concerned a chance was all he needed. It was all he'd ever needed to succeed and this was one matter he was determined would go his way, no matter what.

His finger slid under the flap of the envelope, tearing the adhesive strip away and pulling out the folded sheets of paper. His eyes skimmed the report—assimilating the data quickly before shoving the papers back into the envelope and grabbing his keys off the surface of his desk.

It was time to face Helena with the truth.

As he pulled up outside her house he noticed another car off to the side of the parking bay. The bright red European sports car shrieked money. Had Helena bought the car for herself? If so, what with?

The auditors had presented him with an interim report this morning. Money had been siphoned off systematically for years—starting at about the time Helena had taken up her position there, when Brody had started school. Everything pointed to her, but still he had no actual proof as to who the culprit was.

Something kept niggling at him, though, and begged the question—why had she come to him for help? If she had something to hide he was the last person she should have come to. He knew that it had been Patrick's instructions that had sent her to him. Patrick had to have seen the money trickling away. Maybe he'd even suspected her already but lacked the wherewithal to confront his beautiful young wife. He certainly wouldn't be the first older man to be hoodwinked by a pretty face and a lithe body.

Or the first *younger* one either, Mason reflected bitterly.

One thing was patently clear. Patrick's indulgence of Helena had cost the company dearly.

He wandered over to the car, taking a look inside. A sale and purchase agreement lay on the passenger seat. He picked out the name on the agreement. Evan Davies.

Evan? What the hell was he doing here? Heavy morning dew lay in big round droplets on the showy red paintwork. From the looks of it he'd been here a while. All night?

The money Mason had paid out to Evan would make him a fine candidate for Helena's apparent insatiable financial hunger.

An ugly black rage rose within Mason's chest. Was she still sleeping with him? An even more unpalatable thought crossed his mind—had she ever stopped?

Mason ground gravel beneath his foot as he pivoted and made for the front entrance, ignoring the doorbell and hammering his fist against the heavy wooden door. He forced himself to calm down. What did it matter to him if she was still in bed with Evan anyway? It would only serve to make his case stronger—to give him the additional leverage he'd need to petition the family court.

The sound of someone pounding down the stairs from inside filtered through the door. He heard locks tumbling open, then the door swung wide.

Evan Davies stood before him—hair dishevelled, dressed only in a loosely-fastened robe, with a stain of lipstick on his unshaven cheek. Bile rose in Mason's throat at the thought of Helena's body meshed with this man's. Of her hands entangled in his hair. Of her lips against his skin.

His hands clenched into fists and Mason was hard-pressed not to drive one of them into the smug, sleepy features of the man standing before him.

"I thought I told you to stay away from her."

Evan's smirk widened into a smile. "Can I help it if the woman's insatiable?"

"Where is she?"

"Showering. I was just about to join her. We're both kind of…dirty."

Mason clenched his teeth so hard he thought his jaw might snap. It didn't matter, he kept telling himself. None of it mattered. He'd gotten rid of Evan Davies before, he'd do it again.

"You might like to reread that contract you signed," Mason growled warningly.

"What contract?"

"The one where you waived independent legal advice and sold me your shares to Davies Freight." Mason hesitated a moment before continuing, his voice low and dark with fury. "The one where you agreed to forfeit the money if you went near Helena again."

"That'll never stand up in court." Evan paled markedly.

"Won't it?" Mason narrowed his eyes.

"That clause was absurd and you know it. The lady's fair game."

"Let's just see about that then." Mason reached into his pocket and withdrew his cell phone but before he could flip it open Evan began to speak again.

"Don't bother. I concede. To be honest, she's not worth it. After all, if she was, you'd still be tucked up in her bed instead of hammering at her front door, now wouldn't you? So what happened? You weren't man enough for her that she had to call me back?"

Mason saw red. He took a step toward the other man, his shoulders bunched with suppressed rage. Evan scooted back on bare feet and reached out to the hall table where he swiped up a set of keys.

"Don't waste your energy, mate. Look, I'll get out of here and you can sort it all out together."

Dressed only in a robe, Evan jogged to his car and took off down the driveway, leaving a few feet of twin strips of rubber in his wake.

Mason stepped in through the front door and closed it with a resounding thud. Every instinct screamed at him to take the stairs, two steps at a time, to burst into Helena's room and wipe the remnants of her night with Evan from her body with his own. He thrust his hands into his jacket pockets and rocked on his heels, his fingers brushing the envelope he'd pushed in there on his way out the office. The crunch of the paper reminded him what he was here for.

Brody. *His son.*

"Who's there?"

Helena's voice echoed from the top of the stairs. Mason looked up. Her hair was swathed in a towel and she was encased in a neck-to-ankle thick towelling robe.

"Your lover's gone," Mason said as he started up the stairs toward her.

"What are you talking about?" Confusion marred her forehead with a frown.

"Evan. He just left."

"He's not my lover!"

"No? That's not what he said. And," Mason leaned

forward to flip the lapel of her robe, "given the evidence, I believe him."

"What is it with you? I've already told you, he's not my lover."

"You want to know what it is? I'll tell you. Quite frankly, you disgust me. We all know he's going to burn through that money I paid him for his share in Davies Freight. Is that your plan? Are you going to help him through it? Is your thirst for money so great that you'll sleep with anyone, anytime?"

Smack!

His head reeled back with the slap, his skin stinging from where her fingers had whipped across his cheek. He ran his tongue around the inside of his mouth, the tang of blood where his cheek had been cut against his teeth fuelling his anger.

He reached into his pocket and pulled out the envelope from the diagnostic lab, shoving it toward her. Her hands reached out instinctively to take it from him.

"What's this?"

"The proof you thought you wanted."

"What do you mean 'thought I wanted'?"

"Brody is my son."

Even though she had known the truth, her knees buckled and she reached for the balustrade for support. "I knew it."

"Then you might have considered that before you jumped between the sheets with Evan Davies."

"But I didn't!"

"Let's leave that for the lawyers to decide."

Her face drained of colour. "Lawyers?"

"I'm suing for full custody of my boy. You're unfit to be his mother."

"You're going to try to take him from me?"

Mason leaned so close he could smell the lingering scent of vanilla and cinnamon soap on her skin. "Make no mistake, Helena. *Try* doesn't even enter into it. I will win, and I'm sure Evan will make a convincing witness."

"I did not sleep with Evan!"

"Having had firsthand experience of your appetite, I suppose 'sleep' is a relative term under the circumstances. Oh, and by the way, my auditors have almost completed their investigation. You have some explaining to do. Get dressed."

Helena heard the words but they didn't make any sense. Mason was going to take Brody from her. He couldn't have hurt her more if he'd taken a knife to her body. She remained frozen where she stood as the reality of his claim started to sink in.

Evan had turned up at her house late last night, boastful about his new car and definitely the worse for wear after a meal that had obviously been more liquid than solid. As much as he had revolted her with his behaviour, her conscience wouldn't let him drive home. He would be dangerous behind the wheel of any car let alone the over-powered European import he'd indulged in. She'd suggested a taxi, but instead he'd staggered upstairs and he'd fallen asleep in the first bedroom he'd come across. Unfortunately, that bedroom had been hers. She had left him where he'd lain and locked herself in the guest room at the end of the hall. The one she'd shared with Mason.

She'd barely slept, always keeping a wary ear out for his unwelcome attention and plagued by memories of the night she'd last spent in the room. Eventually, though, she must have fallen asleep, waking groggy when she'd heard Evan up and about.

"Come on, I haven't got all day, Helena."

Mason took her by the arm and led her back up the stairs and to her bedroom. At the door he hesitated and suddenly she knew why. Strewn all over the floor were Evan's clothes. The bedcovers and sheets were tangled over the mattress, one pillow on the floor. A cold uncomfortable chill crept down her back as she felt him stiffen at her side.

"I'll wait for you downstairs."

His voice was arctic. A sense of impending disaster wrapped around her heart and squeezed tight.

"I need to dry my hair so I'll be a few minutes."

"Don't fuss on my account. Your charms are wasted on me."

With that he turned and she heard his footfalls as he thundered down the stairs and the front door opened and closed again. Helena flexed her hand, her fingers still smarting from the slap she'd dealt him. She couldn't believe she'd lost control like that, that she'd actually struck him. With the way things were going, no doubt he'd be charging her with assault as well. She looked again at the paper Mason had pushed at her. The proof she'd wanted so desperately so he would help to get Davies Freight back up on its feet again.

It all came down to the old saying, "be careful what you wish for" in the end. Now she had what she needed—what she'd hoped for to ensure that Brody would never want the way she had, would never have to settle for second best or waylay his dreams for lack of money—she ran the very real risk of losing her son. Fear was an ugly, insidious sensation, she decided as she unwound the damp towel from her hair and reached for the blow-dryer. A very ugly sensation indeed.

Despite Mason's insistence that she not take any bother over her appearance, Helena needed the armour that a formal business suit and full makeup gave her. By the time she made it down the stairs and to the front door she could almost fool herself into believing it would be just another day at the office. Almost.

Mason sat in his Porsche—she could see his fingers drumming on the steering wheel. As she locked the front door behind her and approached the car he leaned across and pushed open the passenger door.

"I was on the verge of coming to get you. Dressed or not."

"It's a good thing I'm ready then, isn't it." She took her time settling herself in the seat and putting on her seat belt. "So what is it the auditors have found?"

"I'm not discussing that with you without witnesses to record the meeting. You'll have to wait."

Helena's brow furrowed.

Mason flung her a dark look. "Worried? You should be. I told you I'd get to the bottom of this. You should have learned to hide your tracks a little better."

It was pointless arguing with him. She'd learned that now. No matter how hard she pleaded her innocence, no matter what she said, he wouldn't believe her. She stared blindly forward, oblivious to the familiar scenery as it whipped by on the journey to Davies Freight.

Why had it come to this, she wondered. Why had it come to the point where she would lose everything she'd worked so hard for? A gaping hollow hole opened in her chest, the ache going straight through her heart.

Brody. How on earth would she be able to fight Mason in court? He had the means, the influence and the support to do whatever it took to win. To take her son from her.

The prospect of saving Davies Freight came a very poor second to the thought that she'd lose Brody.

"We're here." Mason's clipped words penetrated the fog of worry that clouded her mind.

"Fine. I'll be as glad to get to the bottom of this as you are."

"Don't be so sure about that."

His words hung like an ominous knell in the air as they walked across the car park and into the building. At reception Mandy looked startled as Helena came through the door.

"Mrs. Davies. Good to have you back. Are you feeling better now?"

"Fine, thank you." Helena shot a questioning look at Mason as they made their way up the stairs to the next floor. "What was that about?"

"I thought it better under the circumstances if they didn't know you were being investigated. You never know where misplaced loyalties might lie that could jeopardise the investigation."

"My staff are loyal to me because I'm a good employer. Not for any other reason."

Mason didn't respond, instead leading the way to her office. He held the door open for her, gesturing that she should precede him into the room.

A comforting sense of familiarity swept over her as she entered. The pictures on the wall, the bookcase, her desk. All of it reflected her personality. Her framed degree hung on the wall opposite her desk so she could see it and remind herself daily of how far she'd come. Of what she'd achieved. All her life, all she'd wanted was to be able to say she'd made it. Now, it looked like she was going to lose it, too.

She put her bag down and sat in the chair behind her desk, silently staking her claim. She clasped her hands together in front of her, squeezing her fingers tight to hide the trembling that threatened to give away her anxiety. If Mason saw even one sign of weakness she had no doubt he'd be in for the kill and she'd be out of here before she could so much as say the words *balance sheet*.

A knock sounded at the door and a tall willowy blonde walked in, a bunch of reports in her arms, and a smile on her face as wide as the Auckland Harbour Bridge when she saw Mason standing there.

"Mason." She acknowledged his presence with a warmth in her voice that went way beyond professional acquaintance.

Helena fought to quell the swell of envy that rose from deep inside her when Mason turned and smiled welcomingly at the newcomer.

"Ah, Sherie, all ready?"

"Yes, I think you'll be surprised at the results." The blonde flung a look in Helena's direction. "Mrs. Davies, I'm Sherie Watson. Mason contracted my firm to conduct the audit on Davies Freight. I can see why you were all concerned, I just don't know if we're going to be able to act soon enough to bolster things back up."

A young man arrived at the door with another stack of files. Sherie cleared a space on the desk for his armload of information.

"This is Alex, my assistant."

Mason took a step forward and put his hand on Sherie's sleeve. To Helena's annoyance the cool blonde blushed at the contact.

"Is there anything else you need before we commence?" He phrased his question with the type of smile Helena would have walked over hot coals to receive from him.

"No, thanks. We're all ready." Sherie smiled back.

Over the next two hours, Sherie and Alex systematically went through their report and Helena had to brokenly admit to herself that the facts were damning. Within a very short period of time after she'd started working at Davies Freight, sums of money had been filtered through an account—false invoices were being paid. The sums had been small at first, probably so as not to raise any flags with the accountant at Flannigans, who finalised their year-end accounting after the data was initially collated at Davies Freight. But over the past three years the sums had incrementally increased until the company had virtually been haemorrhaging money into one account.

"So it's simple then, track down whose account the money is going to and we have our culprit." Helena pushed her chair back from the desk and rotated her shoulders to work out the kinks she'd gained while poring over the reports.

"We, umm…" Sherie shot a wary glance in Mason's direction. At his nod, she continued. "We believe we know what account the funds have been filtered into."

"So, you know who it is. What are you waiting for? Why haven't you called the police?"

"It's a bit more difficult than that." Mason spoke up from where he'd been leaning against the wall, arms crossed and watching Helena. His scrutiny had made her uncomfortable at first, but once she'd started looking through the reports and listening to Sherie and Alex, he'd faded into the background.

"I don't see what the problem is."

"Would you like us to leave the room?" Alex offered.

"No. I want two impartial witnesses to what I have to say."

"Impartial?" Helena snorted. "They're hardly impartial when they're in your employment."

"Actually, they're not in my employment. They're independent of Black Knight Transport."

Helena settled back in her chair. Whether they were independent of BKT or not, Sherie was certainly not impartial when it came to Mason Knight. Well, she was welcome to him.

"So?" Helena lifted her chin and looked Mason square in the eye. "Who's the thief? Whose account has the money been going into?"

Mason stood up and removed a sheet of paper from his breast pocket. He carefully unfolded it before putting it down on the desk in front of Helena.

"Do you remember this?"

Helena picked up the sheet and examined it. All she could see were rows of figures, none of which seemed to make a great deal of sense. "It's a piece of paper. Why should I remember this one in particular?"

"Perhaps because you'd hidden it behind the photo you were so keen to remove from the office when you were suspended from your duties."

"Hidden it? Don't be ridiculous. The first time I saw that was when you picked it up out of the broken glass."

"I could almost believe you, if not for one thing. Helena, the account the money has been going into is yours."

Nine

Mason watched through narrowed eyes as every last vestige of colour drained from Helena's face. Her green eyes grew huge, the pupils dilated. A fine bead of perspiration raised on her upper lip. From his point of view she couldn't look more guilty if she tried.

"Nothing to say?" he prompted.

"I didn't do it. I don't know where the money's gone but I certainly didn't put it in any bank account in my name." Her hand fluttered up to her throat as her words choked in a voice thick with tears. "Please, Mason. You have to believe me. I didn't do it."

"I'd hoped you'd be reasonable about this, Helena. That you'd have the guts to come out and admit it when faced with the truth. It seems I was wrong."

He picked up the sheet of paper and folded it carefully before putting it back in his pocket. He turned to

Sherie and Alex, both of whom looked uncomfortable at the scene that had unfolded before them.

"Thank you. I think we have everything we need."

"Sure. We'll send through the finalised report once the computer forensics people get back to us in writing—I've been told their information will confirm everything here. Should be sometime tomorrow." Sherie put out her hand to shake his.

When they'd gone, Mason dropped into the chair opposite Helena's desk. She hadn't said a word since her tearful plea, but had remained frozen in her chair.

"I don't want to have to take this to the police, Helena. If you return the money to Davies Freight and formally resign from your position, I'm prepared to leave it there." He lifted a hand to the back of his neck and rubbed wearily at the tension there.

"No."

"I don't think I heard you right." Mason leaned forward. Surely she didn't mean to still deny it. She'd been shown the proof.

"I am not going to take responsibility for something I didn't do."

"You have to admit the evidence is fairly damning."

"Yes, it is, but even evidence can be fabricated. Which computers have you had analysed aside from mine?"

"We did your home computer and the one from the office here."

"You didn't have Evan's computer examined?"

"No need. It wasn't him."

"What makes you so sure? Why are you so prepared to believe that he's not responsible for this?"

"Because, while Evan is money-hungry, he has neither the finesse nor the patience to carry something like this off for so long. If it had been him, he would have simply skimmed off several large sums and gone shopping." There had been some misdealings by Evan— overspending on expense accounts, exorbitant lunches and hotel bills purportedly for company business, but that's as far as it went. Mason could stomach those losses, sure in the knowledge that Evan had no chance to do any further damage to Davies Freight. Helena's activities, however, were another thing entirely.

"Then it was someone else. Someone who had access to my password."

Mason expected to feel anger at her repeated protestations of innocence, but instead, he was devoid of anything but relief it was nearly over. "I'm only glad Patrick didn't live long enough to discover what you were up to. It would have broken his heart to know what you're really like."

"What I'm really like? He knew exactly what I'm really like, which is more than I can say for you and your crazy accusations."

Helena's mind spun in dizzy circles. Faced with the same evidence, she knew she would have come to the same conclusion. It was devastating to realise she had so little to go on—so little with which to prove her innocence. Bit by bit, everything she had worked so hard for during her married life was sliding through her fingers. Her security, her identity—even her very own son. And for what?

What was security anyway? She knew now, for sure, it wasn't tied up in her marriage or her job. Everything she'd ever believed in, had ever put faith in, was systematically shattering about her.

Mason remained silent after her last outburst,

choosing to cross his arms and observe her from across the desk. His very reticence gave her hope. He wasn't immune to her; she knew that with the intimacy of a lover. But would he listen—would he give her the benefit of the doubt? The answer was a resounding no. It was time to change tactics.

"It might surprise you, Mason, but I actually agree with you about Patrick."

He uncrossed his arms and shoved his hands deep in the pockets of his charcoal-grey suit. His body language implied he was open to discussion but the frigid expression on his face told her differently. "Really? You're right, I am surprised. Why start now, Helena? Running scared?"

"Scared? Not me." She shook her head gently. "No. I agree with you in being glad that Patrick didn't live long enough to see this—to see you behaving like this. He loved you like a son, Mason. Like his very own son. And now you're undermining everything he stood for."

"You're being melodramatic."

"Do you think so? I don't. You forget. You may have known Patrick for, what, fifteen years, max? I lived with, and loved, the man for twelve years, twenty-four-seven."

"And were paid handsomely for the job from what I can tell." The curl of his lip was enough to make her want to strike out at him, but she would never succumb to such emotional weakness in his presence again.

"If you think repaying Patrick's devotion to me by loving him unreservedly is something to be ashamed of then I'm sorry, but you have another thing coming. You have no right to denigrate our love for one another, or our marriage." She pushed herself upright, trying to meet him eye-to-eye. "You can do your damned best to try and discover what has gone wrong here at Davies

Freight. You can crunch numbers, you can interview staff, you can lay your unfounded accusations. But you can never take from me the life and the love I shared with Patrick." She paused for a moment, locking eyes with him before continuing, "And maybe that's the problem."

Helena pushed past him and rushed out the office. She'd braved it out long enough, but now she could barely see for the tears that blinded her vision. Tears for Patrick and for Brody, but most of all, tears for herself that she'd managed to fall in love with the one man on the face of the earth who'd never believe in her.

As she tore down the stairs and out the front door she realised that all the things she'd thought came first in her life came a distant second to knowing she loved and was loved in return. And if she couldn't have that love, she would darn well have to learn to live without it. She could rebuild her life and her son's life—brick by brick if she had to.

Suddenly it was clear that all her adult life she'd been barking up the wrong tree. Sure, it was okay to want things. But under everything remained the security of a strong and happy relationship. An equal sharing of life and love and personal philosophies.

She'd had that to an extent with Patrick but, even so, she knew in retrospect that major aspects of their relationship were missing—unbalanced. She and Mason could have those things together, had he been willing. Yet he wasn't. He was so bent on his vendetta against her—against the wrongs he perceived she'd wreaked on him. They didn't stand a chance. Not when he didn't trust her. Not when he didn't believe in her as a person, let alone as the mother of his son.

She only hoped now that she could still retain

custody of Brody. Mason would enter the fray with all legal guns blazing. He'd made his stance perfectly clear. And now, with the financial evidence he'd amassed against her, she doubted she'd stand a chance in any family court. His suspicions now, intertwined with her past, would give him all the ammunition he needed.

A dry, harsh sob shook her from deep within. She could cope with starting over if she had Brody. Surely he couldn't take Brody?

In the crisp, wet winter air she dragged one breath after another into her aching lungs. Eventually the constriction that bound her chest began to ease off, and her breathing came easier. What to do now?

She had to talk to Brody. Maybe, if he was in agreement, she could sell his share of Davies Freight to Mason on condition that he drop the custody proceedings.

But it wasn't Davies Freight Mason was after, a little voice reminded her. It was their son.

Mason raked a weary hand through his short, cropped hair. What a day. Helena had barely uttered a word as he'd taken her home after the confrontation at the office. It drove him crazy that she continued to deny any wrongdoing. He'd have been open to discussion if she'd just been honest with him, but the evidence was damning and yet she still wouldn't budge an inch.

He'd spent the rest of the day at Davies Freight, going over the figures again and again, searching for some clue that might show if she was telling the truth. The truth? Why would he even begin to think that she was capable of such a thing? Sure, she'd argued back, convincingly, that she was innocent. But his deep-seated mistrust of her told him a different story.

One way or another he'd been frustrated at every turn today and eventually he'd given up and headed for the oasis of his own company's offices. He took the elevator to the top floor of the BKT building and his shoulders started to relax. Thank goodness he had staff he could rely upon to do the right thing by him and to keep things running smoothly while he split his days between here and Davies Freight.

The situation at the latter really worried him. If the business was to stay up-and-running it needed a cash infusion and it needed it right now. The thing was, who would be fool enough to get involved when the success or failure of the company was so precarious? His instincts told him it would be best to cut his losses. Wind up the company and absorb only those operations that would benefit Black Knight Transport. But there was more than that at stake.

The company was Patrick's legacy to Brody. Patrick had often said that the boy had an old head on young shoulders and had genuinely looked forward to showing him the ropes. Could he, Mason, honour the wish of a dead man or would he simply be courting financial suicide?

As the elevator doors slid open he was no closer to finding a solution. The lights were still on in his front office and as he entered the reception room of his inner sanctum he could hear the familiar rat-a-tat-tat of his personal assistant's fingers as they flew over the keyboard. Margaret Daniels had been with him since he'd first started the business and she'd mothered him from day one. Now widowed, and with her children grown, she frequently stayed to work late.

"Margaret, what are you still doing here? It's past time you went home."

"Oh, you know it's no bother, Mr. Knight. Besides, you have an unexpected appointment waiting for you in your office." She arched one greyed eyebrow in his direction. "When you're finished, you have some explaining to do."

A sinking feeling settled in his stomach. Had Helena decided to come clean? Was she waiting for him in his office to finally admit to her theft? A piece of him hoped like crazy that he was right and that he could start to put this whole episode behind him, but as he pushed open the door and saw who waited in his office his heart stuttered in his chest.

Brody.

The slender-built boy turned from Mason's desk to face him and it was as if he was looking into a mirror—a mirror from over twenty years ago. The boy's face, above his neatly knotted school tie, was pale but stoic, his chin held high and his black-brown eyes met Mason's full on.

"You're my father."

There was no question in Brody's voice and the shock of those three simple words stopped Mason in his tracks. Behind him he heard Margaret discreetly close the office door. Something which no doubt cost her dearly given the bald statement she couldn't help but have overheard. He'd worry about that later. For now, there was one pressing issue to take care of, yet for some weird reason words failed him.

"I've known for ages, so don't bother denying it. Dad told me just before I turned ten. He said I was lucky to have two fathers, that it was more than some boys ever got." The boy's shoulders squared and he stood as rigid as a post, challenging Mason to respond.

"Yes, it's true. I am your father. I didn't know for certain myself until today." Mason stepped forward and put out his hand. Brody shook it like a man, but the handshake felt all wrong. Mason's arms ached to take his son in his arms, as he'd been cheated of doing for far too many years, and acknowledge the boy as his own. He dropped Brody's hand and gestured to the long settee against one wall.

"Take a seat. We have a lot to talk about. Not the least of which is, does your mother know you're here?"

The boy had the grace to look shamefaced. "No, I— I kind of ran away from school. It's just that I knew something was up. I knew Mum was stonewalling me, trying to protect me from something. The blood tests— they weren't for glandular fever, were they? It was to prove you're my father."

"Yes." Mason sat down next to his son. "We didn't want you to know just yet. Looks like your dad had other ideas, huh?"

"He was like that. Always wanting to be one step ahead, y'know?" Brody's eyes shone with unshed tears as he determinedly blinked them back. "I miss him."

"Me, too. He was a great man."

"He helped start you up, didn't he?"

"Yeah, he did. And he gave me some stiff competition until I diversified, too."

Brody nodded. "He told me that. He said if anyone could beat him at his own game it was you. Are you going to close down Davies Freight now?"

The boy's question shocked him. "Why would I do that?"

"It's your only real road-transport competition. Dad reckoned you would have already done it if he hadn't helped you get started."

It was galling to realise, but Brody's words were true. And he *was* thinking about shutting down Davies Freight, even if for an entirely different reason.

"You won't close it down, will you? I mean, when I grow up, I'm going to run it. It'll be my turn to give you stiff competition."

The thought of mentoring his son bloomed in his chest, but the question of whether it would be at Davies Freight or not had a severe dampening effect. Given the same circumstances he wondered what Patrick would do. Would he fight to retain a flailing business, or would he read the writing on the wall and invest his energy in another direction? The answer eluded him.

Mason looked at his watch. It was late and it suddenly occurred to him that Brody's school would be frantic by now. "I need to call your school. Let them know you're okay."

Brody sat back against the cushions on the couch. "Don't worry. I asked your secretary to ring school for me."

Mason's eyebrows raised in surprise. "And what about your mother? Did you ask Margaret to call her, too?"

Brody squirmed a little in his seat. "No. Mum would only have yelled at me and made me go back before I got to meet you. She's always got to do things right. It was her idea not to tell me the truth about the tests, wasn't it?"

"She thought the news would upset you. She didn't want you to have to deal with it so close to losing your dad." The last word stuck in Mason's throat.

"I'm not a baby! She should have told me!" The boy quietened a little after his outburst, sneaking a sideline look at Mason. "Are you mad at me?"

"To tell you the truth, Brody, I really don't know." And it was the truth. By the time his heart had resumed a normal rhythm he'd simply been blown away by the fact Brody was even in his office.

"Mum'll be mad. I don't suppose we can get away with not telling her?" Brody looked at Mason's face. "Nah, I didn't think so. So, do you want to ring her or should I?"

"Let's just take you home and deal with it then. What do you reckon?"

The boy's face brightened. "Yeah, that's brilliant. She wouldn't dream of yelling at me in front of you."

Mason wondered if that were true. He still vividly remembered the day, not long after his mother had become so ill she could barely move from her bed, he'd taken off from school and raced home. He could still see the joy in her eyes that he'd come to look out for her, but he still felt the sting of her quiet disappointment that he'd left school to do it. She'd ordered him back to class in no uncertain terms. She'd been firm with all three of her boys that way, but they'd never doubted her love for them. Even when she grew so ill that she could no longer leave her bed.

Connor barely remembered that time. Declan had simply gotten on with the basics of looking after the family and their dad had just about worked himself to the point of exhaustion. Through it all, Mason had spent every possible minute at his mother's side. Strange that he should think of that now. Those memories had been supplanted by other more painful ones as time had gone by.

He stood up. "C'mon, let's go. She's got enough on her plate right now without worrying about you."

The lights in the house were blazing as they drove up the drive to the front door. Before the car's engine had even stopped Helena was flying out the door toward the passenger door. She yanked the door open and pulled Brody from the car and into her arms. She hugged him so tight Mason thought the boy would suffocate, before pushing him away from her and holding him at arms length.

"I rang your school to talk to you and they said you'd gone. Oh my God, I was so worried about you. What were you thinking? You know you can't just up and leave like that whenever you want to." There was no mistaking the fear in her voice. The fact that Brody was perfectly safe didn't begin to touch the terror she'd obviously gone through.

"I'm sorry, Mum." Brody hung his head.

Helena stared at her son hard, then shook her head before turning her eyes on Mason.

"And you. Why did you have to get involved? Couldn't you wait before starting your campaign to take him from me?"

"It's not his fault. I went to him," Brody protested. "If you're going to be mad, be mad at me."

"Oh, don't get me wrong, young man. I am thoroughly mad at you. But I'll deal with you later. Go inside, now." Her tone brooked no argument.

Suddenly Mason was seeing a side of Helena Davies he'd never seen before. The lioness with her cub. It was an aspect of her he'd never considered. The front door slammed with a hollow thud as Brody shut himself inside. If anything, his action made Helena's spine stiffen even further.

"Explain yourself," she demanded.

Mason felt the familiar anger that always simmered beneath the surface when he was around her begin to bubble to the surface.

"Explain myself? I had nothing to do with it."

"Don't be ridiculous. You told me this morning you were going for custody of Brody. You had to have talked to him. Why else would he have run away from school like that? Couldn't you have waited? Couldn't you have damn well let me handle my son my way?"

He wanted to argue back, to point out that Brody was his son too. Yet there was an edge to her fury that hovered on a distress so deep it forced him to hold back the words he wanted to shout in defence.

Instead, he spoke quietly. "Brody was waiting for me at my office. I had no idea he'd be there."

"You expect me to believe that? You never just accept what happens around you, Mason Knight—you make things happen."

"I'm flattered by your observation, but in this case you're wrong." Mason looked toward the house just in time to catch the movement of a net curtain in one of the downstairs windows. The boy was obviously watching. "It seems that Patrick beat us both to the gun."

"Patrick?"

"He told Brody the truth just over a year ago."

Helena's face paled in the reflective glare of the outside lights. "He told Brody? Why?"

Mason sighed heavily. "Goodness knows what was behind Patrick's thinking. God knows how he even knew it was me and not some other random guy you might have slept with."

She took a step back as if he'd physically struck her and he instantly felt shame for what he'd said.

"I'm sorry. I shouldn't have said that. It was uncalled for."

"But it's what you think, isn't it? To you, the test

results only confirmed that you are Brody's father, but deep down you thought he was some Russian roulette baby. That he could have been anybody's. Not *just* yours or Patrick's." She crossed her arms defensively across her body, as if by doing so she could somehow shield herself—as if she couldn't bear to take another emotional blow from him. "I didn't deliberately keep the truth from you about Brody because I truly didn't know. You're not the only one that Patrick lied to by omission. We're in this together. We could have something here, Mason. Something special. We already share a child, we could share so much more. But none of that matters, does it? No matter what I say or do, you won't ever believe me, will you?"

Words choked in Mason's throat. He honestly didn't know what to say. Everything concrete told him he couldn't trust her but a tiny niggle in the region of his chest urged him to listen to her words and to seek the truth in them. He hissed an expletive under his breath.

The crunch of her footsteps on the driveway as she walked back to the house told him he'd had his chance to speak and lost it, and with that knowledge came the weight of realisation that with his silence he'd lost far, far more.

Ten

Mason paced the confines of his study in his home nestled on the side of Mount Hobson in Auckland's prestigious suburb of Remuera. The ice in his shot of whiskey melted, unheeded, and the lights reflected in the distance did little to soothe his fractured thoughts.

Just when had Helena managed to creep under his skin so far that he'd begun to think she might be telling the truth? He threw himself into the deep button-back chair positioned by the lit fire and stared, mesmerised by the flames licking and dancing over the wood.

He didn't want to believe she might be right, but again and again her words echoed in his mind.

We already share a child, we could share so much more.

What would it be like, he wondered, to share a life with her? He looked around the study, his hideaway when he was at home. On the mantel he had framed shots of his family and the walls displayed the work of his favourite New Zealand artists. The furniture in here was nothing but the best, like everything he surrounded himself with. But even so, his picture-perfect residence was lacking in the warmth that would make it a home. It was little more than another testament to his success.

He'd worked hard to be where he was today. He'd accumulated so much and now stood poised on the brink of diversifying across the Tasman into Australia as well. After that, who knew? He'd achieved so much in a very short period of time—success many men and women spent a lifetime working for. And for what? To enjoy it on his own?

Mason thought of his brothers. Both workaholics who'd been corralled in the past couple of years by a couple of gorgeous women. Connor had married his secretary, but not without a whole lot of stress on the journey. Declan had married his dead fiancée's best friend. Neither of them had done it the easy way, but both had loved the women involved enough to work past their problems. And that's where he differed from his brothers—he didn't love Helena.

Even as the thought took shape in his mind, his heart thudded painfully in his chest.

Was that the problem? Despite everything, was he in love with Helena? He pushed the thought stubbornly from his mind. He would not go down that road. His father had loved Melanie, or so he'd said when he'd blamed Mason wholeheartedly for the breakdown in that relationship.

But a small voice continued to niggle at him. If he didn't love Helena, why had he agreed to help her? He hadn't wanted to believe her about Brody, and under any other circumstances he'd never have bought into Davies Freight. He'd have done what he'd done with the other smaller companies he'd absorbed over the years and bided his time to make an offer. Then, when they finally stood in a position where they couldn't say no, he would have swooped in for the acquisition. So why was he working so hard to plug the holes and make Davies Freight work?

It was no longer out of any loyalty to Patrick. His mentor had lost that when he'd deliberately hidden Brody's parentage. The words Helena had taunted him with days ago came back to haunt him. The words where she'd made it clear she didn't believe he'd be where he was in his life right now without Patrick's influence. Okay, so that much was true. But the man had stolen eleven years of his son's life from him. At what stage had Patrick planned to tell him—to let him in on the secret of what he was missing?

It was impossible not to be bitter, not to regret the lost years. But hoarding bitterness could only lead to a slow poisoning of the system and eventually to complete shutdown. He'd already learned that the hard way with his father.

Mason studied Tony Knight's craggy brow in the photo and, in his father's face, began to see himself in another thirty years. He didn't like what he saw. A man still driven by the mighty dollar, still driven to hide from the grief of losing the one woman he'd loved.

The woman he loved? Did he love Helena Davies? He'd tried to convince himself she was no more than a sexual release, but sex with Helena had done anything but release him. It had only served to wind his desire for her tighter and tighter, until he was certain no one else could ever satisfy the hunger that grew within—no one but her.

Mason shifted uncomfortably in his seat. Damn, but she drove him crazy—even with just a thought.

The last time he'd felt like this he'd been a teenager and look at the trouble that had gotten him into. He'd been unable to refuse the advances of his father's mistress and in the end his weakness had driven a wedge between him and his dad that still remained.

So was it Brody that drove him to keep Davies Freight alive? No. His son could learn from the ground floor at BKT if he really wanted to. Mason understood how important it was to understand every aspect of the business. And if Brody didn't want to work from the bottom up, that was okay, too. He could provide his son with every opportunity to ensure he could never want for a single thing in his life.

A single thing but his mother.

When he won sole custody—and he was confident he would—how would Brody cope with the change in his lifestyle? Kids are adaptable, sure. But how would three dramatic life changes—losing a father, gaining another, then losing his mother—affect Brody in the long term? Did he want his son to be just like him?

The similarities between them went beyond the physical. Mason had been almost eleven, just a few months younger than Brody was now, when he'd lost his mother. But he knew he wouldn't do to his son what his father had done to him, nor betray him as Patrick had done. Never in a million years.

Damn, but his head hurt thinking about this.

But soon the loneliness he felt would be a thing of the past. There'd been a message on his answer machine from the family law solicitor he'd engaged to petition for custody of Brody. Once he won, he'd enrol the boy in a school here in Auckland, keep him close. Begin to make up for the lost years.

He looked up at the heavy wooden mantel that framed the fireplace, and in particular at the recent photo he had of his dad and brothers. What would they do in the same situation, he wondered. There really was no argument. No matter the circumstances, blood ran thicker than water. Well, at least part of the time.

That certainly hadn't been the case when Melanie had cried wolf, and insisted Mason had been the one to initiate things between them. The atmosphere at home had become unbearable after that night, and the situation had grown even worse after Melanie left. It hadn't taken long to get to the point where Mason couldn't stand the estrangement, or the guilt, any longer and two days after finishing his last year at high school he had walked straight into the New Zealand Army recruitment office and signed up.

His father's farewell when Mason left for training camp had been cold, stilted. They still had too many words left unsaid between them. And all because of a woman like Helena.

Mason lifted his tumbler and took a sip of the warmed whiskey. He grimaced at the watered-down flavour and set the glass on the table beside him.

We could share so much more.

The cynical side of him tried to convince himself that when she talked about "more" she was probably talking about money, but his heart told him different. He thought again of the look on her face—the horror in her eyes—when she'd been presented with Sherie's evidence. Either she'd been giving an award-winning performance, or she really was telling the truth and the account information was completely news to her. Thinking now about that look was enough to make him doubt his own opinion, a fact he wasn't comfortable with in the least, especially since he'd been so driven to find her accountable.

He wasn't the kind of man who doubted himself. But then again, he wasn't the kind of man who normally would unreasonably search for evidence to prove that Helena was the culprit without casting a wider net. He'd judged her guilty based on his feelings for her. Feelings that right now battered against his heart and his head with all the subtlety of a fully laden eighteen-wheeler travelling at a hundred kilometres an hour.

They were missing something. It galled him to admit it but he'd been totally, deliberately, blind to the possibility that someone else was the thief. For goodness sake, the paper had been found behind a photo he'd seen on Patrick's desk himself. It was entirely possible that Helena hadn't even known it was there. It was a possibility that flickered to life like a reluctant flame in his mind—a possibility he hadn't even allowed himself to consider before.

Could Patrick have hidden the evidence there? Surely not. But maybe he knew about the thefts? Perhaps he'd believed it was Helena and had chosen to do nothing about it. Or maybe he'd known it was someone else and was biding his time, waiting for the right moment to expose the thief.

With a sigh of self-disgust, he pushed himself up out of his seat and took his glass through to the kitchen, rinsing it out in the sink before stacking it in the dishwasher. He looked around the room, a room which in most houses was the hub of the home. It looked perfect. It looked as though no one lived there, and in reality, with the hours he worked, no one did. It was nothing like the warm friendly room at Helena's house with potted herbs in the kitchen window and the detritus that showed frequent and comfortable use of an area.

No, this wasn't a home, this was merely what he'd allowed himself to be reduced to. An accumulation of wealth and success in an unconscious bid to prove he was the better man. He'd allowed Helena's marriage to Patrick to drive him into this solitary domain and he'd had enough. It was time to step up to the plate and admit he'd been wrong.

She'd been right on the money when she'd said the love she'd shared with Patrick had been his problem all along. He'd been so driven by jealousy, and by the what-might-have-beens he'd refused to see her for what and who she really was. Worse, he'd allowed his disillusionment over Melanie to sway him to find similarities between the women. Amplifying the flaws in Helena that he thought he'd found, and making himself miserable in the process. His feelings for Helena, no matter how hard he tried to suppress them, had kept him from forming any lasting relationship with another woman. But then he hadn't ever wanted anyone else the way he wanted her.

A single truth shattered through his mind—*he loved her.* No one else would do. No other woman had impacted on him the way she had and now that she was free, he could dare to want her for himself—provided he hadn't irrevocably ruined his chances by his truly awful treatment of her over the past few weeks.

It wouldn't be enough just to have Brody. He wanted the whole package. He wanted them both, forever.

For Helena's sake, he knew know he had to prove she was telling the truth or he would die a very lonely man. He'd treated her appallingly. It was time to make that up to her, if she'd let him.

So far, he'd done everything he could in the investigation to remain above board—the audit, the computer forensics, the lot. Now, it was time to dig deep below the surface—whatever the financial price. If he could find out what had happened to the money when it passed through the account set up in Helena's name, he'd be a giant step closer to finally winning the woman he'd loved for longer than he wanted to admit.

His brothers would help, he was sure of that, and their anonymity in the investigation might be just the leverage he needed.

Ding dong.

Mason flicked a glance at his watch. Ten o'clock. Who the hell visited at this time of night? The doorbell went again.

"All right, all right. Hold on, I'm coming," he shouted as he strode through the echoing house and opened the door.

"Hey, bro'. Nice welcome." Declan Knight turned to face his other brother, Connor. "Looks like we made the right decision to come over. He's alone."

Connor merely eyed Mason from the front step and nodded.

"Too bad if I wasn't, right? Like you guys would just leave if I had company?" Mason fought to keep a welcoming smile from his face.

"I hear you've been holding out on us," Declan

drawled. "Connor tells me congratulations are in order—*Dad.*"

From behind his back, Declan produced a twelve-year-old bottle of Scotch and pushed past Mason. Connor followed close behind.

Standing at the door, Mason spoke to the empty front porch, "Sure, c'mon in, guys." Then, with a sense of rightness he hadn't felt in a long time, he turned and followed them down the hall. His brothers were just what he needed right now. Among the three of them, they'd get to the bottom of this.

And then it would be time to reach out and get the woman he loved, just like he should have done twelve years ago.

Helena saw the real estate agent to the gate, where she hammered a For Sale sign in the grass verge at the front of the poperty. The agent had impressed her with her professionalism and enthusiasm. She'd assured Helena that she had several buyers on her books for the home already. With any luck, she wouldn't even have to endure so much as a single open-home day. The sooner she could get this over with, the better. She wanted everything cut and dried and off her hands.

Two nights ago it had finally occurred to Helena that if she sold the house, as was her right to, she could put back into Davies Freight a good deal of what had gone missing—whether she'd been responsible or not.

She still couldn't understand how so much money had been filtered into an account in her name and then been siphoned off elsewhere unknown—she might never understand it. But one thing she knew without doubt. If Mason Knight wasn't going to save Davies Freight for Brody, she'd do it herself.

The fact that the company was now half Mason's wasn't lost on her. Maybe though, with this act, she could finally get him to accept that she wasn't the money-loving whore he'd all but accused her of being. She caught a glimpse of herself in the hall mirror. Well, she wouldn't attract any punters looking like this. Her face was pale, her hair lank and dull, and her eyes red-rimmed from lack of sleep.

Since that night a week ago, when she'd stayed up for hours watching Brody sleep, she'd struggled through the dark hours. Her breath caught as she thought of her precious boy. He'd have died of embarrassment, for sure, if he'd known she'd remained in his room long after he'd drifted off. But it had been with a sense of fatalism that Helena decided this might be one of her last chances to spend time with her son before his feelings toward her were poisoned by the knowledge that she'd decided not to contest Mason's bid for custody.

When she'd bid Brody goodbye at the train station early the next morning to send him back to school, it had taken every ounce of her courage to remain strong and not break down.

She was confident she'd made the right decision. It was more than her heart could bear to drag her son through her past, and her reasons for marrying Patrick. She was certain she'd have rights to see Brody. There wasn't a judge living who'd deny her that. But she was prepared to stand aside. For now. For her son. In years to come, when he was mature enough to make his own decisions, when he could understand the sacrifice she'd made out of her love for him—out of what was right, for him—she had no doubt he'd come back to her. But if she forced Brody to decide now, or put him through the agony of a family court trial and the push-me pull-you that would come about, she could do irreparable damage.

She strolled slowly up the drive, looking at the garden with a sense of loss that she wouldn't be here to see the newly pruned roses burst into bloom again in the spring, or the tulip bulbs she'd planted last April push through the ground to give a carpet of colour on the edge of the driveway.

The bulbs reminded her of her love for Mason. How there was so much evolving beneath the surface, reaching for the light of day, reaching for the warmth of reciprocated love. But it wasn't to be. She knew they didn't stand a chance together, no matter how much she loved him. In her heart of hearts she knew if she could just set this one thing right, then knowing how he felt about her wouldn't weigh like a millstone about her neck.

Helena looked around her again. She'd come so far from the twenty-year-old bride she'd been when this house was built. She had everything, and yet she had nothing. Nothing but her single-minded purpose to set things right in her world again. No matter what the cost.

It would be worth it, she consoled herself. It had to be.

Eleven

She'd just pulled the front door closed behind her when she heard a vehicle roar up the drive, its wheels skidding slightly as it drew to a halt. At the sound of a car door being slammed shut, soon followed by rapid steps up the front stairs, filtered through the heavy front door, she froze. *Oh no,* she thought, *please not Evan. Not today.*

"Helena?"

Mason? She snuck a peek through the peephole. Maybe she'd have been better off if it had been Evan after all. Him, she could handle. No wonder she hadn't recognised the sound of the car. Behind Mason stood the big black truck she'd crashed on his private road. He'd obviously finally gotten it back from the panel and paint shop. Maybe he was here to give her the bill, she thought, on the verge of hysteria.

"Helena!" She jumped as he hammered at the door. "C'mon. I know you're in there. Open the door."

She made a decision to face him—so she could say goodbye. This time, for good. She took her time turning the key in the lock and only opened the door sufficiently wide to show her face.

"What the hell is this?" Without so much as a hello, Mason pushed the door open and held up the For Sale sign the Realtor had just finished hammering into the ground. Soil from the stakes attached to the sign dropped on the tiled entrance.

Helena crossed her arms and stood firm in the doorway. "Last time I looked I didn't answer to you. I don't have to tell you anything."

Mason's dark eyes narrowed suspiciously. He hurled the sign off to the side of the front porch. "What are you up to? Why are you selling the house?"

Helena sighed resignedly. He wouldn't leave without an answer and if she wanted him off her front porch she'd have to tell him the truth. "If you must know, it's because I won't need it soon. It's far too big for me, anyway."

"Downsizing? That doesn't sound like you." He sounded surprised.

She shook her head. "You don't know me."

You never did, and you never will. The knowledge cut her like a knife. She fought to control the tremor in her voice—she had to hold it together. About now, her lawyer would be calling his to say that she'd chosen not to contest his petition to have custody of Brody. Her insides felt as though they were being torn apart but she daren't give him so much as an inkling of how much this killed her inside, inch by slow painful inch. She lifted her hand to close the door but he was faster and inserted his large frame in the doorway.

"You're right, I don't. But what if I want to?"

"It's too late for that, Mason. Look, if you really want to know, I'm selling the house to put the money back into Davies Freight. Okay, are you satisfied? Now you know, you can leave."

She lifted her hand to the door again, but he held his stance refusing to budge.

"But I'm not nearly satisfied, Helena." His voice was low and rich, like the texture of velvet. "Are you?"

"Don't play games with me, Mason. I'm not in the mood."

"Okay. No games. But do one thing for me."

"One thing. And then you'll leave me alone?"

"One thing, and then, yeah, if that's what you really want, I'll leave you alone."

He was up to something, she was certain, but for the life of her she couldn't gauge what it was. There was a look in his eyes that she couldn't quite define. Surely he would be satisfied she was selling her home to refinance the company. Something didn't sit right with her though, and caution urged her to find out what he wanted before she would agree to anything.

"So what is it?" she demanded. "What's this one thing you want from me?"

Your forgiveness would be a start. The words echoed silently in his head and Mason had to think twice before answering. He'd set this process in place and he planned to follow every step to the letter. No shortcuts. If he got this right, everything would be worthwhile. If he didn't…well, it didn't bear thinking about. Failure was not an option. Not now, not with Helena.

"I need you to come with me." He reached out to take her hand and urged her gently out onto the front porch.

"Come with you? Where?" She pulled back, resisting his gentle coercion.

"You'll find out when we get there."

"Just because I'm paying money into Davies Freight doesn't mean I'm admitting anything. It had better not be a police station you're taking me to, Mason, or God help me, I'll—"

"Don't worry. It's not the police."

"Let me lock up then. Do I need to bring anything?"

"No. We won't be long."

To his relief she turned and locked the front door, slipping the house key in her jeans pocket. The black sweater she wore highlighted how pale she was, and how exhausted. Guilt struck him square in the chest. He'd done this to her—even driven her to try to sell her home. So much hinged on the outcome of the next hour. He hoped like crazy that his instincts had been right and that it wasn't entirely too late.

Mason handed her up into the cab of the truck, and walked around to the driver's side. When he realised how much space lay between them he instantly regretted bringing the larger vehicle. In the Porsche they'd have been closer together. He sensed her stiffen when she realised where they were headed—Davies Freight.

"What are you doing? Why are you bringing me here?"

"There's something you need to see for yourself." He clenched his jaw tight. She wouldn't like what was coming next. It had taken him and his brothers the better part of the past week to nail this. Like anything important, it all came down to the finer details. Now they had the conclusion he'd been seeking all along.

As they pulled up in the car park, Helena swiftly undid her seat belt and alighted from the truck before he could come around and open her door. He watched as she straightened her shoulders and smoothed her clothes and as her face assumed calmer lines. It was as if she was determined to put on a brave face for whatever he had lined up for her inside. Pride swelled inside him. She was so strong. Stronger than he'd ever realised or given her credit for.

"They're waiting for us upstairs," he said quietly.

"Then let's get this over with," she snapped and started to walk toward the front door.

She abruptly stopped in her tracks in the foyer, and looked at him, accusation clear in her voice when she spoke. "Who's this?" She gestured to where his PA, Margaret, was sitting on reception. "What's wrong with Mandy? Don't tell me you've started firing my people."

"Just come on in. I'll tell you everything in a minute."

They crossed through reception quickly and headed up the staircase to the next floor. At the door to Patrick's office Mason hesitated a moment, turning to face Helena and holding both her arms just above the elbow in his warm firm grip.

"Now, you're probably not going to like what you're going to hear, but I want you to know I'll be right by you."

He pushed the door open to reveal the two uniformed police officers standing on either side of what had been Patrick's desk. Mason heard Helena's breath catch as she recognised the person leaning back in a chair in the corner of the office. Mandy. Gone was the friendly and welcoming receptionist she'd grown accustomed to. Instead, a hard and mutinous glare distorted her features.

"Mandy? What…?" Helena's voice trailed away, one hand fluttered to her throat as the truth slowly sank in.

"Go on," Mason nodded at Mandy, who turned her head away from Helena, refusing to make eye contact.

"Okay, okay. It was me."

"Why?" Helena demanded, her voice low, steady and resonating with an anger he'd expected. "Why did you steal from us?"

The other woman snorted and shook her head. "We're the same age, you know that? And from the same background too. I couldn't see why, when I was right under his nose for the taking, he had to go and choose you. Why should you have it all? The clothes, the education, the beautiful house. He should have chosen me.

"I was mad when he brought you into the office, all proud as punch about his trophy bride, so I thought I'd teach him a lesson. Just a little one at first, but when no one noticed I decided to take a bit more."

"Then you started gambling, and that's what strung you up," Mason interrupted in a voice colder than a Southland winter.

"Yeah. I started to take too much and Patrick found out about it."

"That explains the paper behind the picture," Helena exclaimed. "He must have started looking into it just before he died. Why didn't he talk to me about it?"

"I'm sure he would've, given time. He wasn't the kind of man to make decisions lightly. In fact, if I know him, he would even have given Mandy a chance to pay it back—isn't that right?" He fixed his stare at the receptionist who nodded. "But when he died, you thought you could keep going and that no one else would know."

"I had to. I owed too much money." The woman's face crumpled and tears shone on her cheeks.

Mason nodded to the police officers. "Thank you for waiting. You can take her now. I think Mrs. Davies has heard enough."

He waited while they escorted Mandy from the room, then turned to face Helena.

"Are you okay?"

"Okay?" She lowered herself into a chair and dropped her head in her hands. "No, I'm not okay. I can't believe she did that to us. She's like one of the family. And I can't believe Patrick kept it from me. Didn't he think I could cope with the news? She was systematically decimating our company and he wanted to give her another chance?" She shook her head as if she couldn't believe her own words.

The phone rang shrilly on the desk and Mason reached forward and flipped on the speaker.

"Yes, Margaret?"

"Sorry to interrupt you, Mr. Knight, but I have your solicitor on the phone."

Mason looked at Helena. She was shaking from the after-effects of the episode with Mandy. She needed him right now. "Tell him I'll call him later."

His solicitor? Fear slammed into Helena with devastating force as she remembered her instructions to her lawyer this morning. She'd given up her son! And for what? She groaned in despair. What had she done?

Mason hunkered down in front of her, taking her frozen hands in his and heating them between his long, warm fingers.

"I know it's a shock, but you can't feel sorry for her. She hasn't even expressed remorse for her actions—in some weird way she still believes she was totally justi-fied. Don't worry, the police will deal with her from here, you won't have to see her again."

Helena couldn't speak. Mandy's betrayal was the least of her worries. Her world was imploding and all Mason could say was "don't worry"?

"Let me take you home. Will you be okay to walk?"

She nodded, incapable of speech. Her mind was racing with what she had to do next. As soon as she walked in that door back home she would be straight on the phone to her lawyer to countermand her earlier in-structions. She'd been a fool for the last time.

The cabin temperature in the truck was set to high and it wasn't long before she began to feel sleepy. The somnolent sound of the four-by-four's tyres as they hummed along the road made it difficult to keep her eyes open. The past weeks' events had taken their toll and she battled to stay awake, but somehow it was just easier to let her heavy lids slid closed. They'd be home in half-an-hour at the most. That's all she needed, just a short kip to refresh herself and get ready for what was going to be the biggest fight of her life.

Twelve

Mason sensed the moment Helena fell asleep and loosened his vice-like grip on the steering wheel. She looked done in. The purplish bruises under her eyes spoke volumes as to how ragged she'd been running herself. It was up to him to make sure that changed.

Her breathing was low and steady, she didn't look like she'd wake for some time. That was probably best, but he knew if he took her straight home she'd probably coolly flick him off at the front door and that would be it. His chance would be gone. *No.* There was no way he'd settle for that.

They approached the motorway interchange, but instead of going straight ahead toward the suburb where she lived, he made an instant decision and turned onto the southern motorway instead. She needed the sleep, he told himself. He'd handle her anger when she realized he was taking her to his holiday home.

He shifted slightly in his seat, patting his trouser pocket with one hand just to confirm his plans would still work. Yes, it was still there. All he had to do now was get her to agree.

During the two-and-a-half-hour journey he kept checking her to make sure she was still okay, that still she slept. It wasn't until he started up the steep grade of the private road leading to the house that she began to stir.

"Wha—? Where are we? This isn't home." She stretched her neck and rubbed a hand across her eyes. "Mason! Where have you brought me?"

"My home."

She looked around in confusion. "But… No! Take me back. Take me back right now."

"I will, I promise. Look, you needed to rest, it was simpler to just keep driving. Besides, we need to talk. This place is as good as any." Mason pulled into the garage and hit the button to close the door behind them.

"We could have talked at my place."

She sounded madder than a wet cat.

"I know. Look, we'll be back in Auckland tonight if that's what you want. Just hear me out first, okay?"

He got down from the truck and walked around to her side, giving her a hand down. She snatched her hand away from him the instant both her feet hit the concrete garage floor.

"I don't have much choice, do I?" her tone was as acerbic as the expression on her face.

"I'd say sorry, Helena, but I'm not. There are things we need to discuss. After that, well, we'll have to see."

"If you think I'm not going to fight you tooth and

nail for custody of Brody, you can think again. He's my son. Mine!"

Mason didn't answer. This was going to be hard enough without antagonising her further. She followed him inside the house, stalking past him and heading toward the large ranch sliders facing the bay. Her body was rigid with anger, an anger he needed to dissipate.

"Are you hungry?" he asked, checking the upright freezer in the kitchen. He pulled out some frozen soup and a loaf of bread and put them on the bench.

"No. I'm not hungry. Just get to the point, Mason. Why have you brought me here?"

He walked into the sitting room and came and stood behind her. She flinched as he put his hands on her shoulders and turned her to face him.

"Okay, you want to know, here it is. First things first. I want you to know I was wrong. Wrong to treat you the way I did and wrong to threaten you. I was furious when I found out about Brody—I just wanted to hurt you back. I'm not proud of my behaviour, and I hope you can find it in your heart to forgive me for the unfor-givable things I did and said."

"I don't know if I can forgive you. You refused to trust me, refused to even listen to me. I meant nothing to you."

"No. You never meant nothing to me—if anything you meant too much. From the beginning I deliberately poisoned myself against you because I knew if I didn't I would end up doing everything in my power to take you from Patrick. Everything."

Her eyes dilated at his words, the forest green pools consumed by her dark pupils. Her lips parted on unspoken words of denial.

"It's true. You have no idea how difficult it was for me to see you come down the aisle that day—how hard it was for me to keep my mouth shut. I'd already decided I wanted you. I was going to do whatever I could to find you again and there you were. Right in front of me, and completely out-of-bounds.

"It was easier to tell myself that you were a gold digger, just like any other, than to admit how much it killed me to see you married to him, to see you have what I believed to be his child."

"Mason, I…I don't know what to say." Confusion clouded Helena's features.

"I know. Look, let's sit down." He led her to the couch in front of the fireplace and bent to light the paper and kindling set in there. This wasn't going as he'd planned. He'd just wanted to get his confession out of the way and move on. But she hadn't reacted as he'd hoped. She was just as closed to him, just as emotionally distant, as she'd ever been. He added a couple of logs to the kindling and then sat down next to her. Somehow he had to do this on her terms.

He noted with relief that she didn't flinch this time as he came closer. Maybe this wasn't a lost cause after all.

"Helena, I don't want to take Brody from you. But I want to be a part of his life. I'll understand if you don't want me around when you're there, but please, let me get to know my son."

"You're going to drop the custody proceedings?" Her voice came out as a breathless whisper, laced with hope.

"Yes. I couldn't do that to you or to him. I was acting out of anger when I said I'd take him from you. Anger at you, anger at Patrick—but most of all, anger at myself.

"I should have spoken up at the wedding. I should never have let you out of my grasp. But that's my cross to bear. I had some hard truths come to me this week. I finally had to admit that I was the instrument of my own failures. I'm not going to let that happen again. I've decided to make my shares in Davies Freight over to Brody, but in your care until he's old enough to look after the company himself. The money problems we can sort out with an interest-free loan from BKT—though you'll never see a cent back from Mandy, unfortunately. I'll be there to help if you want me to. If you don't, I'll understand."

He searched her face for some sign of softening. Some sign that maybe she believed him.

Helena held her breath and waited. There was more that he wasn't saying, she could see it in his eyes, feel it in the tension that held his body. But he continued to keep it in. Suddenly she realised why. Though it had taken a huge amount of courage for him to open up to her like this, he wasn't about to give her an instrument to flay him with unless she showed some sign of forgiveness.

"It's okay. We can sort out Davies Freight later," she murmured. "So where do we go from here, Mason? What next?"

"Helena, I want you to understand that whatever happens next, it's your choice."

"Thank you." She paused, choosing her next words carefully. "I was going to let you have him, you know. That call you didn't take from your solicitor, it was to tell you that I'd decided not to contest your petition. And I wouldn't have, until this morning when you brought me to hear Mandy's confession. Why did you do that?"

"I learned to listen to my heart."

"You what?"

"I learned to listen to my heart," he repeated. "I finally admitted to myself that I love you, Helena. I had to find out who was responsible for what had happened at Davies Freight, for you. Only for you. If I didn't do that I'd never be able to face you and ask you for a future together."

Helena's heart began to swell with hope. *He loved her?*

"I want to know if we stand a chance, as a couple and as a family." His eyes burned into hers as he spoke, leaving her in no doubt of the truth of his words anymore.

"You want *me,* too?"

"Always. Can you forgive me for having been a complete and utter fool?"

Tears sprang in her eyes and she lifted her hands to his face, drawing him toward her. "Of course I forgive you. How could I not? Can we really try again?" she whispered against his lips.

In response he covered her mouth with his and drew her hard against his body, where she belonged, where she finally felt at home.

His tongue teased her lips open and with a joyful moan, Helena surrendered to his caress. Her body sprang to life, every nerve ending on full alert as their tongues entwined in a ritual of belonging. She pushed her hands through his hair and cupped the back of his head, drawing him closer to her, relishing the strength of him, relishing the knowledge that he loved her.

He dragged his lips from hers and stared into her eyes, the question in them obvious.

"I love you," she said, answering his unspoken plea.

"I will never stop loving you, I never could. You know, I have done many things in my life that I've regretted afterward but I have never regretted that first night we had. Never. How could I? Without it we wouldn't have Brody. Without it, we might not have each other now. Patrick was my salvation from a bad situation in my life. I can't say he wasn't important to me, he was—but you, you were my light. You saved my life and I had no other way to thank you but with myself. In the dark, in the cab of your truck, nothing had ever been as perfect as that moment. You're still my light, Mason. Today, and always."

She slid gracefully from the couch and stood on the soft rug in front of the fireplace facing him, drinking in the masculine beauty of his face, the strong plane of his forehead and the slant of his straight nose enhanced by the glow of the fire in the winter light. His eyes simmered with unspoken desire, making her feel more beautiful, more wanted, than any woman in the world could possibly have the right to feel.

She lifted up the bottom of her sweater and pulled it over her head before letting it drop in a dark flurry to the floor. She reached behind her back and unsnapped her bra, delighting in the torment she knew she was inflicting on Mason as he watched, his lips slightly open, his breathing ragged.

Gently, she drew the straps off her shoulders, cupping the lacy pink fabric to her breasts until the last possible moment before letting the garment drop beside her sweater on the floor. She cupped her breasts with her hands—a spear of want, sharp and true, piercing her body with throbbing desire at the apex of her thighs. Her thumbs ran lightly over her nipples, hard and jutting, begging for a stronger touch. Begging for him.

Helena let her fingers trail down over her ribcage and down to the waistband of her jeans where, unable to control the quake of need that shuddered through her body, she fumbled the steel button out of its loop and rasped the fly of her jeans undone. A tiny shimmy of her hips and they, too, lay in a denim pool at her feet.

Mason emitted a harsh masculine groan, and Helena smiled enticingly as she hooked her thumbs into the waistband of her panties and slid them down her slender thighs. On legs that trembled like a newborn foal's, she stepped out of the pile of clothing and toward Mason's waiting arms.

She almost purred in delight as he pulled her down onto the couch beside him and trailed hot kisses along her cheek, her jawbone, and down her throat, laving at her collarbone and sending shudders of exquisite torture coursing through her.

Her hands fisted in the fine cotton of his shirt as she tugged it free from his trousers, then carefully undid each button, pushing the fabric aside, exposing his hard ridged abdomen and the constricted brown discs of his nipples. Unable to help herself, she lowered her lips, nipping gently at the gleaming tanned skin that stretched across his broad, muscled chest, swirling her tongue around his nipples and taking unprecedented delight in the tremor that rocked him as she closed her lips and pulled, rasping her teeth over the tightened sensitive flesh.

Finally, she pressed her own aching breasts against the heated strength of his body. Mason wrapped one arm around her back, possessively splaying his fingers across her buttocks, the action making her clench her thighs and inner muscles, and sending her desire to a fevered peak. She rubbed herself against the bulging pressure at his crotch, delighting in the uncontrolled spasm the tiny friction elicited.

But she wanted more, needed more. *She needed him.*

Helena unsnapped the fasteners on his trousers and slid her hand inside his briefs. A smile of triumph played across her lips as his impressively evident desire for her jumped against her palm. She closed one hand around him, savouring his silky-smooth texture, his heat, his hardness.

"Wait!" Mason's voice was strangled as he grasped her wrist and pulled her hand away. "If we're going to do this, we're going to do it right this time."

Helena watched, confused—her body screaming for the attention she knew only he could give—as he pulled away from her and reached deep inside his trouser pocket. He withdrew his fisted hand, slowly uncurling his fingers to reveal a solitaire diamond ring, the large square-cut stone radiant in the flickering firelight. Her heart swelled in her chest, her breathing stuttered to a momentary halt and tears threatened to fall as she saw what he held so carefully in his hand.

He reached out for her left hand and slid the ring on her finger. "You *will* marry me."

"Yes." She could barely speak through the lump of pent-up emotion in her throat.

"Now," he said with quiet urgency, lifting her hand to place a hot, moist kiss on her knuckles. "Now it's right."

He shrugged out of his shirt and removed the rest of

his clothing as she lay prone on the wide sofa. Then he lay down beside her, their legs entwining, their bodies urgent to join as one. He positioned himself at her entrance. She was so slick with desire, so hot with need; it was an intense pleasure pain as he began to fill her with excruciating slowness. Helena focussed on his face, on the love she saw reflected there, satisfied to be joined together yet craving more at the same time. And then he started to move, sending wild sensation spiralling from deep inside her as he withdrew then filled her again. Her lips parted and she dragged in a breath. She couldn't believe she could be so lucky as to have this second chance at love—a chance to build a life together with Mason. Silently she vowed never to throw this precious gift away.

Pleasure swelled within her, building stronger, harder, deeper, until she fractured apart with a cry. Mason's hips drove against her, sending another wave of pleasure as he reached his own fulfilment and spilled himself within her.

Mason raised himself slightly and twirled one finger in a thick length of her hair, drawing it to his face and inhaling the fragrance it imparted, a fragrance engraved in his memory as deeply as the feel of her body and the strength of her love.

His voice rippled with emotion as he spoke. "I love you, Helena. You are my life. I'm going to do everything in my power to make sure you know that everyday for the rest of your life."

She reached up and pressed her lips in a kiss against the base of his throat before pulling his face to hers and taking his lips, desperate to impart how privileged she felt that this strong, vital man loved her so deeply.

Against his lips she made her vow, "Thank you. I will never betray your love for me. I promise."

Finally she was where she belonged and she knew beyond a shadow of a doubt she could never willingly hurt him again. She and Mason could continue to build their lives, together, from this day.

* * * * *

Don't miss ROSSELLINI'S REVENGE AFFAIR.
Coming later this year
from Yvonne Lindsay and Silhouette Desire.

Turn the page for a sneak preview of
IF I'D NEVER KNOWN YOUR LOVE
by
Georgia Bockoven

From the brand-new series
Harlequin Everlasting Love
Every great love has a story to tell. ™

One year, five months and four days missing

There's no way for you to know this, Evan, but I haven't written to you for a few months. Actually, it's been almost a year. I had a hard time picking up a pen once more after we paid the second ransom and then received a letter saying it wasn't enough. I was so sure you were coming home that I took the kids along to Bogotá so they could fly home with you and me, something I swore I'd never do. I've fallen in love with Colombia and the people who've opened their hearts to me. But fear is a constant companion when I'm there. I won't ever expose our children to that kind of danger again.

I'm at a loss over what to do anymore, Evan. I've begged and pleaded and thrown temper tantrums with every official I can corner both here and at home. They've been incredibly tolerant and understanding, but in the end as ineffectual as the rest of us.

I try to imagine what your life is like now, what you do every day, what you're wearing, what you eat. I want to believe that the people who have you are misguided yet kind, that they treat you well. It's how I survive day to day. To think of you being mistreated hurts too much. If I picture you locked away somewhere and suffering, a weight descends on me that makes it almost impossible to get out of bed in the morning.

Your captors surely know you by now. They have to recognize what a good man you are. I imagine you working with their children, telling them that you have children, too, showing them the pictures you carry in your wallet. Can't the men who have you understand how much your children miss you? How can it not matter to them?

How can they keep you away from us all this time? Over and over, we've done what they asked. Are they oblivious to the depth of their cruelty? What kind of people are they that they don't care?

I used to keep a calendar beside our bed next to the peach rose you picked for me before you left. Every night I marked another day, counting how many you'd been gone. I don't do that any longer. I don't want to be reminded of all the days we'll never get back.

When I can't sleep at night, I tell you about my day. I imagine you hearing me and smiling over the details that make up my life now. I never tell you how defeated I feel at moments or how hard I work to hide it from everyone for fear they will see it as a reason to stop believing you are coming home to us.

And I couldn't tell you about the lump I found in my breast and how difficult it was going through all the tests without you here to lean on. The lump was benign—the process reaching that diagnosis utterly terrifying. I couldn't stop thinking about what would happen to Shelly and Jason if something happened to me.

We need you to come home.

I'm worn down with missing you.

I'm going to read this tomorrow and will probably tear it up or burn it in the fireplace. I don't want you to get the idea I ever doubted what I was doing to free you or thought the work a burden. I would gladly spend the rest of my life at it, even if, in the end, we only had one day together.

You are my life, Evan.

I will love you forever.

* * * * *

*Don't miss this deeply moving
Harlequin Everlasting Love story about a woman's
struggle to bring back her kidnapped husband from
Colombia and her turmoil over whether to let go,
finally, and welcome another man into her life.
IF I'D NEVER KNOWN YOUR LOVE
by Georgia Bockoven
is available March 27, 2007.*

*And also look for
THE NIGHT WE MET
by Tara Taylor Quinn,
a story about finding love
when you least expect it.*

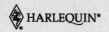

Silhouette Desire

Introducing talented new author

TESSA RADLEY

*making her Silhouette Desire debut
this April with*

BLACK WIDOW BRIDE

Book #1794
Available in April 2007.

Wealthy Damon Asteriades had no choice but to
force Rebecca Grainger back to his family's estate—
despite his vow to keep away from her seductive
charms. But being so close to the woman society once
dubbed the Black Widow Bride had him aching to
claim her as his own...at any cost.

On sale April from Silhouette Desire!

Available wherever books are sold,
including most bookstores, supermarkets,
discount stores and drugstores.

REQUEST YOUR FREE BOOKS!

2 FREE NOVELS PLUS 2 FREE GIFTS!

Silhouette® Desire®

Passionate, Powerful, Provocative!

YES! Please send me 2 FREE Silhouette Desire® novels and my 2 FREE gifts. After receiving them, if I don't wish to receive any more books, I can return the shipping statement marked "cancel." If I don't cancel, I will receive 6 brand-new novels every month and be billed just $3.80 per book in the U.S., or $4.47 per book in Canada, plus 25¢ shipping and handling per book and applicable taxes, if any*. That's a savings of almost 15% off the cover price! I understand that accepting the 2 free books and gifts places me under no obligation to buy anything. I can always return a shipment and cancel at any time. Even if I never buy another book from Silhouette, the two free books and gifts are mine to keep forever.

225 SDN EEXJ 326 SDN EEXU

Name	(PLEASE PRINT)	
Address		Apt.
City	State/Prov.	Zip/Postal Code

Signature (if under 18, a parent or guardian must sign)

Mail to the **Silhouette Reader Service™:**
IN U.S.A.: P.O. Box 1867, Buffalo, NY 14240-1867
IN CANADA: P.O. Box 609, Fort Erie, Ontario L2A 5X3

Not valid to current Silhouette Desire subscribers.

Want to try two free books from another line?
Call 1-800-873-8635 or visit www.morefreebooks.com.

* Terms and prices subject to change without notice. NY residents add applicable sales tax. Canadian residents will be charged applicable provincial taxes and GST. This offer is limited to one order per household. All orders subject to approval. Credit or debit balances in a customer's account(s) may be offset by any other outstanding balance owed by or to the customer. Please allow 4 to 6 weeks for delivery.

Your Privacy: Silhouette is committed to protecting your privacy. Our Privacy Policy is available online at www.eHarlequin.com or upon request from the Reader Service. From time to time we make our lists of customers available to reputable firms who may have a product or service of interest to you. If you would prefer we not share your name and address, please check here. ☐

SDES07

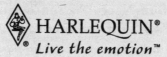

COMING NEXT MONTH

#1789 MISTRESS OF FORTUNE—Kathie DeNosky
Dakota Fortunes
A casino magnate seeks revenge on his family by seducing his brother's stunning companion and daring her to become Fortune's mistress.

#1790 BLACKHAWK'S AFFAIR—Barbara McCauley
Secrets!
What's a woman to do when she comes face-to-face with the man who broke her heart years before…and realizes he's still her husband?

#1791 HER FORBIDDEN FIANCÉE—Christie Ridgway
Millionaire of the Month
He'd been mistaken for his identical twin before—but now his estranged sibling's lovely fiancée believes he's the man she wants to sleep with.

#1792 THE ROYAL WEDDING NIGHT—Day Leclaire
The Royals
Deceived at the altar, a prince sleeps with the wrong bride. But after sharing the royal wedding night with his mystery woman, nothing will stop him from discovering who she really is.

#1793 THE BILLIONAIRE'S BIDDING—Barbara Dunlop
A hotel heiress vows to save her family's business from financial ruin at any cost. Then she discovers the price is marrying her enemy.

#1794 BLACK WIDOW BRIDE—Tessa Radley
He despised her. He desired her. And the billionaire was just desperate enough to blackmail her back into his life.

SDCNM0307